APOLLO'S PROTECTION

GODS REBORN - BOOK TWO

CLAIRE MARTA
ANNA EDWARDS

Sara,

Avoid Camp 71

Anna Edwards

Cover Design by www.CharityHendry.com

Editing by Tracy Roelle

Formatting by Words into Butterflies

Proofreading by Sheena Taylor

Map of the island known at Pluto's Camp Seven

BLURB

Is it possible to escape a hell's paradise and find love at the same time?

Fontus and Eva are demigods of the sea. For years, they've been lovers and friends, but something has always been missing. When both find themselves kidnapped and sent to Pluto's breeding camps, to help him create an army, can they escape the magical island where nothing is what it seems? And will it give them insight into what their relationship needs to survive?

Apollo is the quiet son of Jupiter, unless he's playing his music or making love. He's given a task by his father that he thinks is a fool's errand — a silly little girl hiding from her father for no reason. It becomes so much more, though, when he finds himself on an island full of lovers, forced to breed the army from Hell.

Can the three find a way not only to escape from hell but love at the same time?

Apollo's Protection is a modern day, fantasy, paranormal story based upon Roman mythology. You shouldn't always believe the history you were taught, because the reality can be completely unexpected.

EVA

Prologue

The warm waters of the Mediterranean Sea lap at my feet while I lie in a tiny red bikini on the shores of the island of Sicily, close to Masala. In the distance, I can see the hazy lands of Tunisia. It's a place I swim to often for the exotic spices and jewelry it has to offer. That's definitely one perk to being the daughter of Neptune, the God of the Sea, an ability to swim for miles like a fish. To dip your head under the water and not resurface until you reach your destination is bliss.

There's so much beauty in the shores off the coast of Italy with it's sunken wrecks teeming with fish of all different colors. Many a trinket or fortune can be found amongst the wooden structures, waiting for man to discover. I touch at the necklace I've worn since my tenth birthday, fifteen years ago. Well, in human years. In god years, I'm probably approaching twenty million years old, give or take a few thousand years. Not a wrinkle line in sight, though!

My skin prickles as though someone's watching me, but when I look around, I see no one. Strange? Maybe it was time I was getting back home. Ever since Fontus, my best friend and lover, disappeared, I've been on edge. It's so unlike him not to leave word if he's going away for a while. He's been known to vanish for days on end, lost in his explorations of wrecks, but he always tells me before he goes gallivanting. This time, I had no word. He just didn't show up one day.

I've told my father, and he says he's looking into it, but I think he believes I'm worrying over nothing. He has the same philosophy as a lot of the male gods, which is that some time away and buried deep inside a woman of their choice is essential. Well, I can tell you now if Fontus is doing that, then it'll be the last time he's able to use his dick for those sorts of activities!

I snort out an annoyed puff of air, and jumping to my feet, I bend over, lift up my teal colored towel, and wrap it into a small ball. As I begin to tuck it inside my rucksack, the sky darkens. There's a single black cloud in a bright blue sky. It's eerie—it doesn't seem normal. The hairs on the back of my neck stand up. I need to get home ... *now!*. But I'm too late. My body's frozen in place, and when I try to take a step, my legs won't obey my brain.

"She's pretty, Boss." A deep masculine voice comes from behind me, but I can't turn my head to see the face of the person speaking.

"Indeed, she is." Another voice comes from the left of me. I have some movement in my eyes, and they're able to flick to the side to see a big brute of a man looming over me. A menacing grin full of lust crosses his face. "Very pretty. Neptune should keep her better guarded."

I turn my attention to the sea and will it to save me. A shot of water bursts out of the ocean and heads to the man next to me, but he holds a hand out, and the water stops and veers off to his side.

"Feisty as well. Just how Pluto likes them," the brute to the left continues.

My ears prick up at the mention of that feared name. I've been taught to stay away from any mention of it since birth.

"What do you want?" My voice trembles.

"Well, apart from your body, you're going to make a perfect addition to my camp."

I swallow deeply, wanting to do nothing more than run away.

"But a demigoddess? She's no Venus," the voice questions from behind me.

"No, but in many ways she's better because nobody'll miss her, especially with us holding her part-time lover hostage as well. They'll think the pair have gone away together," the man to the left of me chuckles evilly.

"Fontus!" I cry, but my words are lost on the wind as we disappear into nothing.

APOLLO

Chapter One

"Why do I have to be the one to do it?"

Arms folded over my chest, I glower at the old man facing me. Jupiter, King of the Gods, sits behind the desk with his salt and pepper hair neatly styled and wearing a pinstriped suit that's elegant and smart. He's the head of one of the largest law firms in Rome, and the protector of mankind. He's also my father, and right now, the biggest pain in my ass.

"Apollo, Mars is away on his honeymoon with Vicky, and your other brother is already on an errand for me. There's no one else I can task with this."

No one he wants to ask more like. There are plenty of other Gods working under him in the office. One of Neptune's daughters decides to run off, playing hooky, and I get stuck with chasing her.

"You do know she's probably off partying with a bunch of humans," I point out. "On Ibiza or some other island where they like to get rowdy."

A smile flickers across his lips, his dark eyes crinkling at the corners in response to my annoyance.

"It should make it easier for you to find her then. Her father is worried, and he wants her home. We can't afford to have a young demigoddess running around alone. You know Pluto will stop at nothing to destroy mankind and turn as many of us as he can to his cause. This girl would be easy pickings."

The heat of my irritation cools. He's right. With Pluto, God of the Underworld, forever scheming and plotting, we need to be careful. There have been too many times where he's come close to succeeding. Something we can never allow.

"All right, I'll find her," I concede, knowing my evening with a pretty brunette and a handsome male I'd planned to wine and dine will have to be put on hold. No threesome for me then. Work before pleasure and all that. If I'm lucky, this little sea demigoddess won't be hard to find. After I've reprimanded her, she won't be so naive as to wander so far from home again.

"Good." Pushing a folded piece of paper toward me, across the surface of the wooden desk with his index finger, Jupiter leaves it in front of me. "This was her last known whereabouts. Start from there and see what you can find."

Snatching it up, I read the tiny black writing, and my eyebrow lifts with interest 'Sicily' where there's plenty of beaches, clear waters, and good food. She has excellent taste. This wasn't where I'd expected to start my search. The few of Neptune's daughters I've met have all been selfish and vain. I doubt this one will be any different.

"Hopefully, this is just an instance of a young girl off having some fun." My father's soft voice draws me back from my musings. "But be careful, my son. The forces of darkness are insidious. If Pluto does have a hand in this, we need to know."

Hooking the end of my thumbs in the pockets of my

jeans, I give him a cocky grin and move for the door. "You're getting paranoid, Father. Pluto's just been taken down a peg or two, thanks to Mars. He won't be in a fit state to move against us anytime soon, and you don't need to worry about me. I'll be back in no time with this wayward mermaid."

"If you need any help, contact your sister Diana. She is Goddess of the Hunt, after all, and you could use her tracking skills."

Swiveling on my heels at the mention of my twin sister, I pull a face. "I'd rather spend an eternity in the Underworld than seek help from her."

My father's brows crease with a disapproval I know only too well. "You two used to be so close when you were younger ..."

"And then we grew up, and I realized how truly irritating she can be."

Before he can answer, I walk out the door. I don't need *the* talk about getting along with my siblings, or how our mother will be disappointed. When you've lived as long as we have, you don't always get along with family.

The lovely blonde secretary I'd seen on the way in flashes me a shy smile. As the light bringer, radiant and beautiful, I've never had problems drawing lovers, Gods or humans alike. Plus, I may be the God of Music and Poetry, but my prowess in battle isn't any less intimidating than my brother's. Reaching for a piece of paper with her long, pink painted nails, she scribbles down some numbers with a pen.

"My number, *Signore*, if you would like to go out for a drink one evening." A sweet pink blush sweeps over her cheekbones.

I return her smile, amused at her boldness. There's a

policy against dating staff members, but obviously the attraction I invoke in her overrides common sense.

"Grazie."

Pocketing the note in my shirt, I give her a wink. Never lacking in bedmates, I doubt I'll give her a call. From what I know of her, she's efficient at her job and a hard worker. If I break her heart with a one night stand, my father will have my balls. Entering the elevator, I wait for the doors to close before I teleport myself with the power of thought to the Mediterranean island where I need to start my investigations.

*   *   *

Heat from the summer sun beats down on my head and shoulders as I take in the scenery surrounding me. The Sicilian beach is secluded. Crystal clear azure waters lap at the pristine sand, and Tunisia lies off in the distance beyond the expanse of blue. It's a peaceful cove away from tourists— a place of solitude and silence. It appears untouched, and there's no indication anyone has been here recently. My steps leave an imprint as I trail slowly along the stretch of paradise, examining the shoreline. My disappointment is sharp when nothing turns up. This demigoddess isn't going to make it easy. Wherever she's sunning herself, it looks like she's already moved on from here.

It's then something shiny catches my eye. Half buried beneath the sand—it glitters in the sunlight. Curious, I crouch down, and digging my fingers into the silky softness, I rescue the object that has captured my attention.

A necklace.

Not a cheap trinket, but a valuable piece of jewelry

crafted meticulously from gold and jewels. Old and well cared for. Whoever owned the piece has looked after it lovingly. It isn't something that would be parted with easily. Foreboding coils around my insides. My thoughts of a gallivanting wayward demigoddess become tainted with something more sinister.

Perhaps, this time, my father was right.

EVA

I'm a sun lover—I've always been that way ever since I was a little girl. My father would often find me in the middle of the ocean, lying flat out on the surface sunning myself. It is vastly different to the darkness we usually experience under the sea. Magic glows in the depths, but it's not a natural light. I long for the sun after a few days under the sea—I pray for it now in the gloom of my depressing prison.

It's been three, maybe four days, possibly even longer since I was taken by men loyal to Pluto. I'm scared and alone with little food or water. They've spoken of Fontus a few times, but I've not seen him. Why am I here? Pluto's reputation precedes him, and whatever he wants from me will not be good. I curse myself for being stubborn and not listening to my father. I wonder if people are searching for me?

"Which one does he want today?" a voice calls from down the corridor.

"Number three," another replies from farther away.

"Three, three, three," the first man sings and rattles the doors of all the rooms.

I quickly learned I wasn't the only girl being held captive here. The soft whimpers and pleas throughout the night are nothing compared to the silence when everyone goes quiet and sleeps in exhaustion. Silence is eerie and more poignant in its emotional destruction.

"Three." The man finishes his singing.

No, please don't be me, but I'm not lucky enough for that. My door rattles as someone unlocks and opens it. A man with the body and head of a human but the tail and ears of a horse enters. I've never seen anything like him before. He carries a large staff with him.

"Up, number three," he orders, but I'm too scared to move. "I said up," he repeats slowly, his tone laced with the promise of menace if I don't obey. My legs shake, but I manage to stand.

"Where am I going?" My voice quivers as I speak.

"It's time for your inspection." The horseman curls his lip up into a sneer, and it turns all the blood in my body cold. "Now."

He holds the staff up and prods me in the stomach. I'm still wearing the small red bikini I was taken in, so it doesn't give me much protection against him.

"Ok." My wobbly legs carry me toward the door. The only food I've been given to eat since arriving here is bread, and water the only drink. I'm weak, and every step I take is leading me to an unknown fate. "Where are we?" I ask the guard.

"An island off Tartarus. A magical place full of everything our glorious leader needs."

He pokes me again with his stick to get me moving quicker.

"Stop doing that!" I turn and glare at him.

"Why? Is Daddy going to come and tell me off, little rich girl?"

"He'll do a lot more than that. Ever wondered what it's like to drown on dry land?"

I bring my hand up, and curving my fingers around, I link myself to the water within his body. I don't have many abilities—I'm only the daughter of a god and a human. My powers are virtually redundant against purebred gods, but this thing in front of me is not a god. As I twist my fingers around, I know the water in his body is swelling. It will grow and grow until he drowns in his own skin. Before long, he starts to gasp, and my lips curl into a smug smirk.

"How do I get out of here?"

"Never," he chokes and drops his staff to claw at his throat.

"Which way?" I shout and rotate my hand, allowing more water to flow into his lungs.

He opens and closes his mouth like a fish struggling for air. I wait for his answer, but I never get one, because more guards appear, and I'm forced to release the spell when they shoot me with electric blasts from their staffs. Electricity doesn't mix well with water and agonizing pain shoots through me. I sink to the floor and use my hands to clutch at my body, trying to protect it.

"Foolish girl." One of the newly arrived guards kicks me and drags me to my feet. "Pluto will see you suffer for this. Nobody escapes the island."

I'm weak and in so much pain that I don't really register being dragged along the corridors of the dark prison and out into a large room. Creatures that look like men line the walls —they aren't human, though. I don't know what they are, but they don't move, not even a blink. It's unnerving, and I want to escape even more. I'm thrown onto the floor, and the staffs are pointed at me again to keep me there.

"I have to thank you, Orca. I like them feisty. She'll be perfect for my program." A deep voice fills the room, followed by the booming laugh of another.

"She gave us a good fight when we took her. A beauty from the oceans—a daughter of Neptune no less," the man called Orca replies.

Orca, a scary looking man, places his hand under my chin and lifts it, so I'm forced to look up at both men. My heart tells me instantly who the other man is in the room. Shrouded in the darkness of his position as leader of the Underworld, Pluto stares back down at me. He's my father's brother and my uncle, albeit via adoption. Neptune does not share blood with Jupiter and Pluto despite the human world thinking he does. It's a story that's been wrongly told for a long time.

"Perfect." Pluto motions for me to stand, and I'm roughly handled to my feet. I want to call forth water to drown them all, but I know I can't. I'll be beaten down before I get a chance. "Remove her bikini Orcus."

"What?" I spit out at him.

Orca strips me naked before I have a chance to react or protest further.

"Beautiful." Pluto casts his lustful gaze over my body, taking in every inch and curve. I'm not a small girl. I fill out a bikini, but I do like to exercise and take care of myself, so my body has often been commented on as pretty. I shake my long brown hair to try and give myself some coverage over my breasts, and my hands move downward to cover my neatly trimmed pussy.

"What camp do you suggest we put her in?" Orca questions and retrieves a clipboard from one of the creatures lining the room. "We need more in three and seven."

"Hmm." Pluto strokes his chin, his lecherous gaze still on my body. He reaches out and shifts the hair covering my breasts. Wrapping his hand around my sensitive flesh there, he tests the weight of my tit. I try to pull away, but one of the guards holding a staff behind me sends a bolt of electricity into my body, and I scream out in pain.

"What powers does she have?" Pluto asks his associate, and Orca flips over a sheet of paper. *What the fuck is going on?*

"Mainly water related: drowning capabilities, teleportation, fast swimming."

"Any energy abilities?"

Orca scans down his list.

"Not diagnosed. She's still developing. Neptune has kept her sheltered."

"Is she a virgin then?"

"What the hell? How dare you talk about me like that." I make to slap Pluto's face, but I'm stopped by his strong hand.

"I'll talk about you as I want, Eva. I own you now."

"Nobody owns me," I defiantly inform him.

Pluto laughs in my face.

"Foolish girl. You've no idea what your future holds." Pluto grabs me as he speaks and pushes me into a side-room that appears to be an office with a large desk in the center. He presses a button on the desk and a screen materializes on the wall opposite. It shows a room containing four women at various stages of pregnancy. "If Jupiter thinks he can stop me by taking gods and goddesses away from me, then I'll show him. I can still be victorious by creating my own. This, Eva, is what you're here for … to breed my army."

"I'll never do that." I try to escape from him. But my vulnerability to his plan is already evident from my naked state. "What kind of monster are you?"

"The kind who's the King of the Underworld." He licks up the side of my face while one of his hands trails lower toward where I'm desperately trying to cross my legs together.

"I'll never submit to you," I whimper, tears pooling in my eyes.

"Then I'll take you by force." He whirls me around and lays me out over his desk. His erection digging into my backside.

"*Please*," I cry out, and he presses another button on his desk. This time, the face of my lover, Fontus, appears on the screen. He looks tired and weak. He's covered in blood and appears to be digging in the middle of nowhere with a crowd of people. I don't understand. What is happening to him?

"I think you know who he is don't you?" Pluto leans over and whispers into my ear.

"Fontus." A tear drops from my eye and pools below me on the table.

"Orca, I think it's time to see if she really intends for me to take her against her will," Pluto instructs the other man.

Orca disappears and reappears next to Fontus on the screen. People scatter, but Fontus remains where he is, and apart from briefly glancing up, he continues to dig as if Orca means nothing to him.

"He refused to help create my army. The future goddesses of the Underworld need the power from the surface in them as well. This is his punishment—it's designed to break him and make him submit. Maybe I don't need him anymore now I have you."

"No," I scream as Orca grabs Fontus by the collar of his tattered shirt and throws him to the floor. Orca then balls up a bolt of energy in preparation to throw it at my friend. In

Fontus' weakened state it will injure him badly, possibly even kill him. I can't let that happen. *"Please,"* I beg.

"You know what you have to do." Pluto rustles with his pants behind me, and I know that he's removing his dick from its confines. I don't have a choice.

"I'll do whatever you want," I cry. "Just let me see him. Please, let him go."

"Nobody leaves, but I won't kill him, yet."

Pluto presses another button on his desk.

"Take him to camp seven. Eva will be along after I've finished with her."

"As you wish, sir." I see Orca's response on the screen. He flattens the energy ball, and it disappears into nothing. The screen goes blank, and I'm speared in the next instant by Pluto's hard cock. It's beyond painful, but I have to take it if I'm going to have any chance of seeing Fontus again.

FONTUS

Chapter Three

Confusion numbs my brain. Weak. Hurt. The thoughts shifting through my mind are short and fleeting. I don't remember where I am or how I got here. The one thing I do recall is the male who is currently standing over me.

"Move." His words are as menacing as his ugly face. Hulking, muscular, he's bigger than any of the other men I've seen. They all fear him. He radiates an aura of unforgiving hate and evil.

I flinch with the echoed memories of painful, cruel, brutal fists meeting my body when I fought him previously.

"Please." Crawling to my knees, I try to rise only to stumble and fall back down. Stones cut into my palms already slick with blood and blisters from my toiling. Darkness reigns around us, pierced only by glowing white orbs that hang motionless and radiant, providing us with enough light to see to our tasks.

Laughter rings out above me. "Pathetic. A minor god groveling on the ground like a half-starved dog."

A god? I don't know what he's talking about. Everything before I woke up here is a blank. I don't even know my own name. Put to work with the other slaves, I have no idea why I'm being punished or what I did to warrant my imprisonment. Huddled together, the other prisoners watch on with terrified eyes—their emaciated bodies are clothed in nothing but dirty rags and makeshift garments they've scavenged from those too weak to work.

Finally managing to gather some strength, I rise to stand before him, shivering with the sharp chill in the air.

"Who are you? Why am I here? What do you want with me?"

"You'll remember soon enough once the waters of Lethe we made you drink wear off. Even with your powers, you couldn't stop them from making you forget." A rough, large hand grabs my shoulder. Dragging me forward, his head dips down, so he can stare intently into my eyes. "You'll beg for another sip into oblivion when you do get your memories back, and you won't be the first."

My memories have been wiped? Frowning, I try to grasp something on the edge of my consciousness that weaves in and out, eluding me … a name. The beauty of a smile. Soft and warm … a voice as it whispered over my skin under the heat of the sun.

My jailor chuckles. "Try not to strain something in there. Not that it matters if you do. I think you'll be more accommodating now we have your pretty little playmate."

I meet his pitiless gaze. His expression drips with smugness.

"Playmate?"

"Eva." He says the name slowly as if it's somehow important to me.

Eva? Anxiety spirals through my chest, but I'm not sure why. Some unknown subconscious reaction to a woman I have no memory of. I fear for her—that's clear. They have her—that's also clear.

"There we go." His lips curl up in an unpleasant grin. "Something's stirring in there. She'll be joining you in camp seven once Pluto's finished breaking her in."

"What do you mean?"

"He gets first taste of every female we bring through here. The desk in his office is his favorite place to fuck them. He's gotten quite attached to that piece of furniture."

Rage consumes me fast and raw. Before I even realize what I'm doing, my fist finds his square, unyielding jaw with surprising force. His head snaps to the side with the blow, but it doesn't take him down.

Tongue snaking out, he licks at the trickle of crimson from the cut on his lip. "We're going to have fun with you two. Maybe I'll let you watch when we get one of the others to impregnate her. She might enjoy watching as we breed you as well."

Exhaustion at my show of defiance has me wilting. I have nothing left to give. All my strength is drained. The hand clutching my shoulder transfers to the back of my neck in an unforgiving grip, and the air shifts around us.

One moment, I'm in the cold of a black and harsh world —the next, a warm breeze caresses my skin. Swaying in disorientation, it takes a second to find my bearings. Lush vegetation lies in abundance around us, exotic and green, and a multitude of flowers bloom in bright splashes of color. The heat of the sun is welcome as it beats down from above. What looks like a hotel is nestled in a clearing. The white painted building is grand and Victorian in style. It's so out of place in the jungle surrounding it I have to blink twice.

"Welcome to camp seven." Thrusting me forward, my captor sets my tired legs in motion toward the structure. "There is no escape. If you try, you'll be hunted down and punished. If you are a repeat offender, then we'll strap you down permanently and breed you like an animal in a laboratory."

Long strands of grass tangle around my legs as we walk up the path, hindering my movements. "That's sick and twisted," I spit at him, wondering if what he's telling me is true. This place can't be inescapable. There has to be a way to get off.

"It's the method we used when we started, but we've found better results from letting our stock copulate in a more natural way."

Their stock? Others like me? The thought sickens me. I don't understand their motives. The misery they're causing. Why do they need us to breed?

Eva.

Whoever she is, she must mean something to me, considering the despair I feel at the knowledge this is her fate too. Will I remember her when I see her? Can I keep her safe? She's already been violated by Pluto ... whoever that is. What else has he done to her? Have they taken her memories just as they stole mine? How can I prevent us both being used and bred? Panic and worry churn inside me. I don't protest as I'm directed into the waiting building.

APOLLO

Chapter Four

Taking the steps two at a time I make my way up the narrow stairs. Photos and paintings of old cemeteries grace the deep ruby-red wallpaper. The aromatic smells of cigars and spices are thick in the air.

New Orleans.

Miles away from where I should be looking, but the one sure place I know I can find answers. So far, every lead I've had has come up empty, and for some reason, I can't shake the feeling I'm running out of time.

Stepping through the open door, I take in the room. Masks of all descriptions are hanging from the walls. Strings of colored beads have been draped from hooks. Glass jars filled with herbs crowd a table, interspersed with white skulls. Stitched together with material and buttons for eyes, several voodoo dolls lay scattered on a rocking chair. The sounds from a half-closed door draw my attention. From the groans and moans, the occupants are having themselves a good time. Pushing the door open with my foot, I discover a couple in the throes of foreplay. Spread out on midnight-blue satin sheets, an ivory skinned beauty arches her spine, her luscious breasts thrusting temptingly into the air. Her hair, the color of deep red strawberry wine, spills out over the pillows. Between her legs, her dark-skinned lover looks just as fine as he pleasures her with his mouth. They're unaware of my presence. So lost in passion and the moment, nothing else exists.

Leaning my shoulder against the doorframe, I cross my arms and watch the show. I'm tempted to join them. Lose myself in the rapture of their youthful, flawless flesh and find a heady bliss. Work before play and all that. I need to find this demigoddess before my father starts breathing down my neck. I've come here for Selene's help.

A soft cry emanates from the bed, a faint flush infusing the skin of the redheaded beauty as she comes. Trailing kisses up her thigh, the young man moves to cover her with his naked form.

"Sorry to spoil your fun, and as much as I'm enjoying it, we need to talk," I interrupt.

Startled, they both jump at the sound of my voice, and with lips parted, their gazes swing toward the door.

"For fucks sake, Apollo, you almost gave me a heart attack," Selene snaps. Gathering a blanket off the bed, she tosses it to her lover, who's now kneeling above her. "Cover yourself, Theo."

Hastily wrapping it around his hips, he throws me a look of anger and distrust.

"Who the hell is this?" he asks with an American twang in his accent.

Slipping into a white cotton dressing gown, Selene leaves the mattress in a hurry.

"An old friend."

"Very old friend," I tell him with a quirk of my lips. "Known her family for years."

Rolling her eyes at me and raking her red locks out of her lovely face, Selene takes Theo's muscled arm.

"Trust me, Apollo isn't going to take no for an answer. Why don't you get dressed and go down the street and buy us some beignets?"

Theo collects up his clothes, and she plants a kiss on his lips before fussing him out of the room. I move inside as he goes begrudgingly to do her bidding. Closing the door with a click once he's left, she turns and leans against it.

"What do you want?"

Sliding my hand into the pocket of my pants, I fish out the necklace I'd found on the beach. "I need you to tell me where the owner of this is."

She eyes it as if it's something poisonous that might bite. Tightening the belt of the robe more securely around her slender figure, she pads to a cabinet.

"And what are you willing to give in exchange?"

There's always a charge with oracles. Not many seers exist, and they all have a hefty price when it comes to acquiring the use of their talents. Selene is the best I've discovered. Gifted with sight beyond all others in her line of work, she's never let me down, yet.

Rifling through a drawer, she finds a cigar and a lighter. Bringing one end to her lips, she lights the other end before taking a drag. I watch the smoke curl up into ribbons above her, the smell is strong and potent.

"What do you want?" I counter while hooking a thong that's been discarded on the end of the bedpost and dangling it in the air.

One eyebrow rising faintly, she's not affected by my charming smile.

"A favor to be carried out at a later date."

It's against my better judgement to agree, but for some reason I can't fathom, I find myself doing just that.

"Fine."

Abandoning her cigar in an ashtray on a cabinet next to her, Selene comes toward me to collect the piece of jewelry. Taking a seat on the edge of the mattress, she holds it between her delicate hands. The precious jewels twinkle in the sunlight streaming in through the window. Eyes closing, her expression becomes blank.

Dropping the thong on the floor, I wait patiently for a vision to find her. I understand to some degree what she experiences. Part of my many gifts is to see prophecies. It's not something I experience all the time, but when I do, it's like being hit with a planet. Days of pain follow and flashes of things sometimes I'd rather not see.

Unease ripples across her features. "She's in a very dark place. So much fear and hopelessness around her. Pain ..."

"Where is she?"

Crouching before Selene, I observe as her shoulders tense. Then straining backward, her whole body vibrates with agony as she writhes.

"Things are changing ... I see a jungle ... things lurk among the trees. There's a building that's not all that it seems."

"Selene, I need a location."

Teeth sinking into the plumpness of her bottom lip, her eyes move rapidly behind the lids.

"An island ... she's on an island."

I know better than to touch her. One distraction and whatever she's connected to could break the fragile chain. It's something I'm not willing to lose.

"Do you think you can tell me where?"

"There's something about the place ... there's magic like

I've never felt before." Eyelashes finally fluttering up, Selene slumps, and the length of her hair tumbles forward, shielding her face. "I can try. But, Apollo, I sense danger and death even for creatures like you."

Standing, I stalk over to the cabinet to retrieve her cigar.

"You don't need to worry about me, Selene. I'm old enough to take care of myself."

Taking her cigar with a shaking hand when I offer it to her, she inhales a long puff before letting the smoke escape through her puckered lips.

"You may be a god, but you are not invincible, my friend."

She's right. We aren't invincible, but I haven't lived this long without picking up some wisdom and tricks along the way.

EVA

A warm breeze blows over my face as I'm left alone in camp seven. I'm naked, having lost all my clothes to Pluto's explorations. I'm sore, and I can feel the evidence of his attempt to breed with me, trickling down my legs. I can only hope it hasn't worked. The thought brings bile to my throat, and I lean down and bring up the sparse contents of my stomach in a nearby bush. I want to go home. Why is this happening? Having been given details of which path to follow, from the guard who left me, I stumble blindly through the trees until I finally find my destination. A white painted building, grand and Victorian in style, looms high above me. No doubt it's here as the result of a god with a penchant for the gothic— it's not something that fits in with the surrounding jungle area. A tree house would be better. At this precise moment, though, I'm beyond caring. I just want a nice warm bath to wash away the dirt covering my body from Pluto.

The door to the house opens, and a face appears I never thought I'd be happier to see. My legs give way, and I fall to the floor as Fontus runs out to meet me. His long legs eat up the distance between us, and in no time at all, I'm cradled in his arms and being carried into the house and toward a bedroom.

"Hold up." A tall figure stands in front of us. His voice sends shivers down my spine. It's laced with the same malevolent incantation as Pluto's. My head is whirling around, and I can't quite make out his face, but I know it will be spiteful and full of lust if I do. "You need to follow the rules. You only just got here. We get first sample of any new meat."

The man tries to tug me out of Fontus' arms, but he holds me tightly.

"You touch her, and you die. She's mine. Inside this place and out," Fontus threatens.

The man laughs.

"Not part of the deal. What happened on the outside world doesn't belong in here. Now take her to my room." The man pulls at me again.

"I said no," Fontus growls at him.

"Big mistake. You're weak from working the rivers. If you think you can take me on, then you have another thing coming," the man continues.

"Fontus." I try to dislodge myself from my lover's arms in a desperate move to prevent him from getting hurt, but his grip is so tight it's bruising my delicate flesh. "Let him do what he wants with me. He can't be any worse than Pluto."

I try to reason with him, but his stubborn streak is one of the things I like about him. We've been friends and eventually lovers ever since I can remember. It's not a forever just yet. There's something missing, but neither of us will admit it.

"Not happening, Eva."

Two more men arrive, and I'm pulled from Fontus' arms.

"Bring them outside," the man who's been demanding me orders the other two. "She can witness what the pecking order around here means."

One of the men carries me while a weak looking Fontus is dragged out of the building by the other two. He's no match for them in his current state—any energy he did have was expelled in carrying me as far as he did.

"Let her go. She's not going to be your plaything. That isn't what Pluto wants." Fontus stands up bravely to the man, who appears to be the leader, while the other two men surround me with lustful looks. Fontus continues, "He wants relationships formed to breed strong children."

All three men laugh.

"Pluto couldn't give a fuck how he gets the children, just as long as he gets them. He wants his army. The cum dripping down her legs already tells me he's tried breeding with your girlfriend. Shame he never seems to succeed. In camp seven, I'm the father of the most children. I'm Invidia. I'm the personification of the envy you all have. I produce the biggest, the strongest, and the most children."

The man beside Fontus reveals his name. He's not a god but a sin—one of the seven deadliest. If my demigod lover was at full strength, Invidia's power would be inferior.

"You mean you produce the most monsters—they're not humans or gods with abilities to fight for what is right," I spit out at him as he bares down on Fontus. My friend, my partner … he's barely able to hold himself up.

Invidia laughs at my comment, and then pulling his fist back, he punches Fontus square on the jaw. Somehow, Fontus doesn't fall. He stands rigid as if planted to the spot.

"No!" The scream leaves my mouth as a shrill sound, sending birds scattering high into the sky. "Leave him alone. I'll give you what you want."

"No, she won't," Fontus interrupts me and receives another bruising thump to his face. He still doesn't fall. The men on either side of me start to run their hands over my body.

"Hurry up and deal with him, Invidia. This one's going to be a good lay. So much better than the other well-used pussy we have here."

I notice several women poking their heads out of windows from above. A couple have men with them, and from their tangled hair and pinking cheeks, you can tell they've been fucking. I won't submit to this. I can't. I have to save Fontus and get out of here.

Invidia continues his assault, but my lover doesn't fall. He stands steadfast although I can tell he's fading. Out of the corner of my eye, I see something glistening in the lush gardens surrounding the house. A pond … salvation. Calling the demigoddess inside me, I summon her powers to control the natural life giver. The water from the pond swirls in a whirlpool before flying through the air and splitting into three. Each jet of muddy liquid heads for its intended target and smashes into their face and up their noses. My power is weakening. I don't know if I have the strength to push it further, but I have to try. I'm the daughter of Neptune.

The remaining strength Fontus has entwines with mine and forces the water down into the men's lungs. They're not gods. They have nothing to match our strength or to fight the liquid bubbling and drowning them on dry land. The two men touching me are the first to fall, gasping and choking. Invidia succumbs last, the envy imbued in his name demonstrated in the way his eyes bulge out of his head in shock at what I can achieve. He thought he could mess with goddesses and break them, but not this one. I step forward, and twisting my hand, he dies before me. He'll live for eternity in the Underworld now as a wandering soul. I have no remorse for my kill though. I drop to my knees beside Fontus. He is weak but breathing.

"Go, Eva, find the ocean. If you can get to it, then you can out swim any creature here. You are the King of the Sea's daughter."

"I'm not leaving without you."

"*Eva*," he pleads.

"I'm not leaving without you," I repeat my declaration and help him to his feet. I inhale deeply, searching for the scent of the ocean, and it instantly unveils itself in my nostrils. "This way."

I start to drag him along with me supporting as much of his weight as I can.

"Eva, you have to save yourself. If you help me, then we'll both die."

I stop and stare flatly into his sunken eyes. "Then we'll both die."

FONTUS

Chapter Six

My face feels like it's about to peel off. Invidia certainly knows how to hit. Shame he never stood a chance of felling me. I've dealt with far worse from my father, not that anyone knows. It's a secret I'll take to the grave with me. I'm glad Eva was able to use her powers to drown the men. My brain wasn't exactly working properly when it came to thinking of a way out. I saw red when Eva stumbled into the yard of the house. Pluto will die for what he did to her. I won't rest until he's rotting in his own personal hell, or as we call it … heaven. No, that would be too good for him. He needs to be obliterated from existence.

"We have to hurry." Eva helps me to travel farther into the woods. I can smell the sea from here. Its calming presence soothes my pains.

"Eva, leave me," I plead with her again, but it falls on deaf ears. She just holds me tighter and continues to drag me with what little bit of strength she has left.

"That's not happening—I've already told you. Stop arguing with me and concentrate on moving faster."

"I don't remember you being so stubborn," I tease her, and she rolls her eyes at me.

"Let's just say I've had a few weeks to develop my anger.

I thought you were off with the mermaids, chasing their tails. I was ready to castrate you a few hours ago. I know differently now, and we're going to get out of here and tell my father what's happening. He can then drown this island, so nobody has to be a breeding mare at Pluto's whim again."

"I think I like this new you even better than the last one. Does it still shop?"

We push through a dense area and into a clearing full of fruit trees.

"I'll always shop. I'm good at it."

I'm struggling with the effort of escaping. My head is spinning, and I'm on the verge of collapsing. Working by the river for so long has withered my muscular form into a pre-pubescent boy's frame. I need something to eat, or I'll not make it much farther. I pull Eva to a halt.

"Can you hear anyone following us?"

She shuts her eyes. I know she has superior hearing inherited from her father. He can hear a pebble drop into the ocean in Hawaii when conversing with dolphins off the coast of Africa.

"No, it's silent at the moment."

"I need to rest a few minutes."

"Ok." Eva helps me to sit on a rock and reaches to pull a bunch of bananas out of a tree. "Eat these. They'll give you strength."

"Pluto's going to be pissed you killed his top breeder," I lament ruefully while peeling back the skin of the potassium laden fruit.

"He can go suck monkey balls. I honestly don't care."

Eva sits down next to me and rests her head on my shoulder. She's still naked, and I feel bad. But wearing little more than a pair of tatty shorts myself, I haven't any clothes to offer her.

"Did he hurt you badly?" I ask.

Eva goes quiet, and I can tell she's composing herself.

"I'll recover." She strokes her hand over her flat belly. "I just hope he didn't succeed in what he was trying to do."

Looking around the clearing, I see papayas. An old wives' tale my mother once told me springs to mind.

"Eat papaya." I nod my head toward the fruit.

"What?" Eva looks at me like I've gone insane.

"Apparently it helps prevent pregnancy."

She raises an eyebrow at me.

"How hard did Invidia hit you?"

"Very hard. Now eat the papaya. My mother told me about it. "

Eva pulls herself up from the rock and reaches for one of the fruits. She breaks it open and scoops out the flesh inside.

"If this stops me falling pregnant with Pluto's child, I'll willingly eat a hundred of them every day." She pops a bite in her mouth, and I can tell she's not eaten one before by the face she makes. "Oh my god that is disgusting. It smells like old feet and doesn't taste of anything."

I laugh at her, my shoulders shaking up and down in amusement.

"But it'll stop you getting pregnant."

"Please tell me that there is something else that will do the same but actually tastes half way decent." She reluctantly takes another nibble and screws up her face.

"I'm afraid not."

Eva stills, her head switches direction to where we came from.

"We need to get moving," she says, and dropping the fruit,

she's over helping me get to my feet in seconds. We push deeper into the jungle, the thick branches scratch our delicate skin. I can smell the sea. I know it is close now. I will my legs to continue, but they are weak, and I'm not sure how much farther I can go. Water, I need the water.

"Quicker." Eva is panicking now.

Whatever she senses coming for us is getting closer.

I'm moving using strength buried deep within my psyche. I don't know where it's coming from, but it's there, and it's going to save us both. The jungle clears, and we see the sea. It's beautiful. Ahead of us is a horizon full of wave after wave of crystal blue salvation. My legs give way. I can no longer stand. Eva drags me over the last vestiges of grass and onto the sand. The smell of it gives me hope, and I push on, crawling along the hot speckles of glass.

A loud crack sounds above us and then a screech that curdles my blood. The sky darkens, and I know magic has caught up with us.

"Leave me," I plead with Eva again, but she persists in dragging me. I'm barely conscious. My arms and legs have no control over where they go. All I can focus on is the sea, but I know I'll never reach it.

"Eva, go. Save yourself," I shout again.

"No," she yells back, and the screeching grows louder.

I can't move anymore. I use my last burst of energy to roll onto my back and see dark shadows circling above us. A creature of my nightmares sweeps down from the sky with its large feathered wings, and its body covered in the scales of a lizard. Its beady eyes warn of punishment for those who try to escape. These flying beasts are the reason nobody leaves the island, not Pluto's guards.

Eva swipes her hand, and a jet of water spurts from the sea and sends one of them tumbling into the trees.

"Fontus, come on." My beautiful girl is crying, tugging hard on my arm, but I'm immobile now. I'll die here on this beach, but at least I know she'll be safe.

"Eva, it's too late for me."

"Fontus. I love you."

"I love you too. Go. Find your father. Tell him everything."

"I can't. Please."

Another bird swoops and receives the same treatment from Eva.

"Go."

I twist my head and look over to the water's edge. Reaching out my hand, I try to will it closer to us, so it can cover her and sweep her away, but my magic is already dead.

Eva kneels down and kisses me on the forehead.

"Thank you,"

Another bird descends, and I know it'll catch her if she doesn't go immediately.

"Now," I shout, and leaping to her feet, she sprints as fast as her legs will take her to the sea. I watch everything while black swirls at the edges of my vision. She's close, so very close. She just needs to get a toe into the sea, and she'll be safe.

The last thing I see before darkness claims me, though, is the creature grabbing her and carrying her away from safety.

APOLLO

Chapter Seven

Cutting the engine to the speed boat, my narrowed gaze sweeps out over the endless stretch of shimmering blue ocean. These are the coordinates Selene predicted. According to her vision, there should be an island here. All I've seen is a pod of dolphins. Pushing the dark sunglasses more firmly up the bridge of my nose to shield my eyes from the glare of the sun, I frown.

Selene has never been wrong. In all the years I've known her family, none of them have made an error. Casting my thoughts back, I go over our conversation. She'd mentioned magic. Could the island be cloaked?

With that idea in mind, I turn the key, setting the boat once more in motion. If it is invisible, I need to be careful. The hazard of reefs or rocks could lay ahead, invisible to the eye. It would only take hitting one to sink me. It also begs the question as to why anyone would go to such lengths? What's so important it has to be hidden?

The cool ocean breeze caresses my skin as a trickle of sweat trails down my bare chest toward my abs. In an open white shirt and a pair of loose shorts, the sun beats down on my already bronzed, muscled limbs. Watching for anything suspicious, I'm almost caught off guard when things turn treacherous. One moment, I'm among gentle lapping waves —the next, I'm caught in a storm.

"What the fuck?" My voice is swept away on the raging wind.

The biting chill of the frozen rain sends shivers over my flesh. I'm soaked through in seconds. Battling for control, my boat is seized in the frenzied tempest. Above, the once clear blue sky is thick with grey ominous clouds, and lightning streaks overhead. Violent waves thrash the hull, rocking it from side to side, threatening to tip me over. Wiping salt water from my eyes, I cast a look out for any signs of land. There's nothing but the sound of the howling, driving wind, and the sight of the dark, dangerous, churning sea. No shelter. No salvation. No time to think.

A roar breaks through the chaos. Turning my head, I glimpse the powerful tsunami right before it hits me. Airborne for a heartbeat, something slams into my body before I can teleport myself to safety.

* * *

Consciousness filters in slowly. Huffing in a breath, silky sand touches my lips. Pain throbs through my temples as memories surge. The last thing I recall is the clutch of the icy water. Eyelids flicking open, I take in the empty stretch of shoreline. Azure waters lap soothingly against the golden sun kissed beach. Farther back, trees with thick green leaves and bright blooming flowers herald the start of a jungle. Moving my heavy limbs, I wince at the ache. Every inch of me feels battered and bruised. If I'd been human, it would be my corpse washed up. Luckily for me, being a god, I'm not so fragile. The moist sand cushions my frame, and my curling fingers sink through the cool grains when I flex them. I doubt the boat made it. By now, it's most likely a wreck on the ocean floor. Whatever magic is cocooning this island, it's strong and savage. In place to keep out the curious and unwanted strangers.

Bracing my upper body on my forearms, I lift myself carefully. There's no sound save the waves. Glancing either side of me, I scope the deserted expanse of land. There's no hint of civilization. Nothing to mark any signs of intelligent life. If my wayward demigoddess is here, then perhaps she's hidden too or in hiding? Rolling to a sitting position, I check in my pocket— relief relaxes my shoulders when I find the necklace is still there. It's precious to its owner. Returning it is something I feel the urge to do although I'm not sure why. I've a driving need to see it worn.

"Where are you, Princess?" I mutter to myself, rising to my feet.

Shirt damp and shredded, it's hanging uselessly off my muscular frame. Stripping the rags off, I check over my shorts. At least they're intact, but I'm missing one shoe. Discarding the other, I leave it abandoned. I have an island to search. Focusing on the tree line, I frown when I don't tele-port. It's an unsettling sensation, and not one I'm used to. I've never been without the ability to travel using the power of thought. Palming the back of my neck, I concentrate again.

Nothing.

"Son of a bitch." The words are spoken low as my mind whirls with unpleasant thoughts.

Leaving this place has just become ten times harder. Selene's warning slithers insidiously into my head. I've been arrogant enough not to inform my father where I was going.

Instead of leaving him the information, I came without backup. No one save the oracle knows where I am. Sighing, I pad toward the jungle. I'm going to have to search the place the old fashioned way. What should take a handful of hours is going to take days. Getting the fuck off the island will be a problem I can solve later. Right now, I need to find the female I'm looking for.

The air is fragrant with the scent of flowers. Birds take off into the sky, startled by my presence. They're colorful plumes create dazzling splashes among the foliage. This place is a paradise. An untouched jewel. Music, the essence of my powers, sounds differently here. The natural noises of nature that sustain my abilities aren't the same here as in the outside world.

Whatever spell or incantation the island is steeped in, it has to be powerful to render my teleportation useless. Apprehension dances down my spine. All this beauty hides something more sinister.

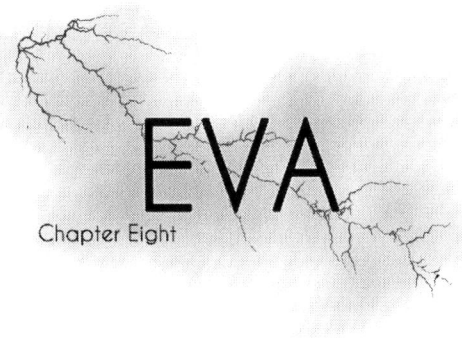

EVA

Pluto was indeed unimpressed that his chief breeder had been murdered. He took me against my will again. His little dick not hitting any sweet spots. The first time I was scared, but this time I was frustrated because all I wanted to do was get back to Fontus and check on him. After he had his fun, Pluto had my water abilities limited, so I couldn't drown anyone else. I was returned back to the house, and after a quick trip to collect some more papaya, I've been seated in the room Fontus and I commandeered as our own. It's in the top of the house, and away from the other rooms where the noise of sex emanates from. The room is sparsely decorated but has a massive bed which Fontus is currently spread out on, the white sheets damp with the sweat of a fever. His wounds seem to be taking forever to heal. I'm sure the salt of the water we usually swim in is what heals us when we're at home. I asked for a bucket of salt water to be brought to me, but the guard laughed at me and walked off. A few of the other breeding men have come in to try and talk to me, but I made it clear I'm not interested, and my reputation, thankfully, precedes itself, so they've left with their dicks tucked between their legs. All I need now is for Fontus to wake.

Pushing myself off the chair, placed next to the bed, I

meander wearily over to the window and move the light-weight drapes aside to stare at the lush jungle outside. I can't remember the last time I had a good night's sleep. I'm uncertain how long Fontus has been this way, but it must be approaching three days at least. My body aches. I'm sore in my muscles from running hard and then sitting constantly. I long for the sea, or water of any sort, to swim and be free in.

A groan comes from the bed behind me, and I spin around to see Fontus' eyes flittering between open and shut.

"Fontus." I race back to the bed and grab his hand. He opens his eyes and looks at me before shutting them again.

"Eva," he moans, his voice cracking from lack of use. I pick up the glass of water beside the bed and place it at his lips. He drinks and pushes it away when he's had enough. "Where are we?" The chirp of crickets outside the window answers his question before I have a chance to confirm: we are still at Pluto's breeding camp. "You didn't make it," he says, opening his eyes again. Lying there in the bed, he's weak and looks a lot older than his twenty-seven years.

"I tried." I feel a guilt weighing heavily on my shoulders. If I'd run just a little bit faster, I would have made it, and we might both be back in the safety of my father's seas.

"This island is cursed." He breaths heavily. His skin still feels clammy from the fever that arose as his body fought to repair itself.

"It's because it belongs to Pluto," I respond.

"No … the strange birds … the magic." Every word is an effort for him, and he drifts between the realms of consciousness and the dream world again.

"Fontus." I place my hand on his chest. "Please, tell me how to help you."

He's always been a fountain of knowledge when it comes

to the nature of the world. I admit I'm the foolish girl who longs for trinkets and a good tan.

"Please, Fontus." My head falls forward so my lips touch his, and I plead with a kiss on his dry, cracked lips.

He groans and tries to shift in the bed again.

"Ginger ..." He breathes the word back into me, his voice strained. "Honey and lemon ... all natural ... will help. Mix and feed ... me ..." The last word is too much of an effort, and he falls silent again except for his labored breathing made visible by the irregular rise and fall of his chest.

Leaning forward, I press a kiss to the top of his head.

"I won't be long," I tell him and grab a spare sheet from the bed. There isn't an abundance of clothes here for me to choose from, so tying the top of the sheet around my neck, I make it into a sort of dress to cover my body.

Thankfully, the house is empty when I leave, or should I say everyone is occupied. I don't encounter another soul that I need to kill.

"Lemon, ginger, and honey," I repeat to myself. Checking the kitchen first, I find some honey and a bag in one of the drawers. I place the honey inside it and look around. It's not a big kitchen and is a mess. There isn't much food in the oak paneled cupboards. I've lived off papayas for the last few days, so I've not really thought about what's available to eat. Walking into the next room, all is explained. Lined up on a side wall are buffet style cabinets with a selection of meals from extravagant chicken and fish dishes to roast beef dinners and mini fish pies. Accompanying vegetables and carbohydrates come next. Lastly, there's a cabinet filled with fruit, chocolate, yogurts, and various cakes. I spy a chocolate cake, and my stomach rumbles, desperate for something more nourishing than papaya. I look around wondering if we are permitted to take the food. I'm expecting to have an electric shock run through me as punishment when I reach out and grab a slice of the cake. It doesn't happen though, so I shovel it into my mouth and moan with delight at how delicious it tastes.

"Is there anything else I can get you?" A feminine voice asks, and catching me unaware, it causes me to almost jump out of my skin. Spinning around, I see an older woman dressed in chef's whites.

"N-no, this is g-good," I stutter. Then spying a lemon, I grab it and put it into the bag.

"Interesting choice." The lady raises an inquiring eyebrow at me.

"My friend is sick. He needs something to make him feel better."

"The new man." The lady comes forward and picks up another lemon and hands it to me. "Anything else he wants?"

"Ginger," I blurt out.

"I don't have any in the kitchen at the moment, but there's some growing behind the house." She opens my bag and looks inside it. "I better add honey to my shopping list."

"I'm sorry." I go to give it back to her, wondering how I can get some more.

"Keep it." She reaches out and touches my hand. It's a comforting gesture, and I warm to the old lady, who's obviously a mother figure in the house. "If you need anything else, just ask. It's my job to keep you fed."

"Thank you."

I grab a handful of grapes and head to the door but stop when she calls out to me.

"Don't try to stop Pluto. As soon as your friend's well enough, get him to give you a child. It will make you safer.

Take it from someone who's known what it's like to live here all her life." She turns away from me and goes back into the kitchen—her shoulders are slumped in defeat. I couldn't imagine spending all my life here. She'll probably never recover from the horror she's been through here, it must have left deep rooted scars. I can't think about that now, though. I need to find the ginger and get Fontus well. Until he's awake, I'm vulnerable to the other men, and we're not able to figure out a way to escape this place and return to the sea.

The rest of the house is a blur as I walk through it and outside into the heat of another summer's day. I wonder where this island is. I thought my father, with his knowledge of the seas, would be aware of all such places on Earth, but he's never spoken to me about a magical island like this. I would have explored it before now and probably gotten myself into a lot of trouble … as I'm in right now.

I eventually find the back garden where the ginger grows. There are rows upon rows of the flat leafed plants that I know, when pulled out of the ground, reveal roots that will help me cure Fontus. I tug hard at one, and it pops out of the soil. I break off the green leaves I don't need and brush off as much dirt as I can. I'm about to go back to Fontus when a dark shadow looms over me.

"Eva."

I look up to see a handsome blond man staring angrily at me. He's dressed in only a pair of shorts that have seen better days. His muscular chest takes my breath away—its curves are like a marbled vision of a god on display in a museum. He grabs my hand as my brain catches up with my body, and I kick him. My foot goes straight into his knee. He curses and lets go of me.

"Haven't you lot learned your lesson yet. I'm off limits. Touch me once more, and I'll kill you just like I did Invidia." I prepare to storm back into the house, but he grabs me again —this time, being careful to keep his distance, so I can't hurt him.

"I'm not in the mood for games, Princess. I don't know what the fuck you're doing here, but it's time to go back home to Daddy," he spits at me while I struggle against him.

"What?" I freeze.

"You heard me." He digs into his pocket and produces my necklace. I stand there staring at it and gasping.

"Who are you?" Tentatively reaching out, I take it from him, a powerful surge of strength cascading through me as I'm reunited with my spirit of the sea.

"Apollo. But until we get the hell out of this place, don't tell anyone. This island is eerie." He looks around warily like he's expecting something to jump out at him. "Why you chose this place to have your diva tantrum is beyond me."

I place a hand on my hip and stare up at him. I've heard of Apollo—he's one of Jupiter's sons.

"You think I want to be here? I've tried to escape already, and now my friend Fontus is upstairs almost dead as a result."

Apollo pulls me to him. He's on his guard constantly, and it's scaring me because as a full god, he's extremely powerful. Little scares a purebred god.

"We need to leave."

"Well teleport me to Fontus, and we can leave from there in the same way. I'm not going without him," I order, but the way his eyes flick to the side uneasily tells me it won't be that simple. "You can't teleport, can you?"

He shakes his head, telling me no.

"What is this place, Eva?"

I slump back against a nearby brick wall.

"It's Hell on Earth. Welcome to camp seven of Pluto's breeding army." I place my hand on my stomach. "Where if you're lucky, you'll die in childbirth because it's the only way you'll get off it."

FONTUS

Chapter Nine

It feels as though I'm being seared from the inside out. Moaning through dry, cracked lips, I fling my arm over the side of the bed. I've no idea when Eva left. Time is drifting brokenly as I slip in and out of consciousness. My fevered mind is a whirlpool of past and present. Half-forgotten dreams edged with half-remembered nightmares. I crave the cool relief of the water … the ocean. A longing to dive deep into the endless blue and touch the sandy bottom. Will we ever reach its safety again? Find our way home?

A hand touches my face. Groaning at the shock of coolness, I flinch as a large palm presses against my forehead. It hurts.

"His fever is raging." A male voice I don't recognize says to my left.

"I was collecting herbs to make him a tonic to bring his temperature down when you found me."

Eva.

Concern is thick in her sweet, young voice.

Cracking open my heavy eyes, I focus on her where she's standing at the end of the bed. A man is beside me. Sitting on the edge of the mattress, his handsome face is carved in worry.

"Who?" I manage to get out hoarsely.

"Apollo," he replies. "Eva's father asked for help in locating her. I had no idea there were more of you. Now lay still," he advises when I try to sit up.

The god Apollo. Relief washes over me. Jupiter, the King of the Gods, will have an army on the way to save us all.

Eva moves closer, her gaze flicking between me and Apollo. "Can you help him?"

"Yes. I have the power to heal although for some reason my abilities seem to be limited here." He frowns.

Whatever magic holds this place in its sway, it has effected all of us. That realization sends a tremor through my body.

"Easy now," he soothes, mistaking my reaction as a consequence of the fever. Crawling onto the bed, he urges me to roll onto my side. Confusion swamps me, but I obey without protest. Lining himself up, he snuggles against my back. I'm aware of a muscular chest, strong legs tucked behind mine, and an arm curling over my waist.

"What the hell are you doing?" Eva's voice is full of disbelief.

"I told you something is interfering with my powers, which shouldn't be possible. If I'm going to heal him, I need as much body contact as possible."

From her expression, I can see she's not sure what to believe. I know she's torn between her anguish for me and an urge to escape.

Moving my hand weakly on the sheet, I pat the place in front of me. "Lay with me, Eva."

Without hesitation, she quickly moves to join us. Brushing my sweat soaked hair from my cheeks, she cups them gently. "Please get better, Fontus."

Her eyes bounce between mine, shimmering with unshed tears. She's been so brave. Endured so much. Pluto will pay for what he's done to her.

Pressing my lips to hers, I kiss her. It's an innocent gesture, filled with hope and the love I feel for her. Energy gathers along my spine. Tingling, dousing as it spreads through the fire of the fever alight within my system. With it comes a pulse of desire. Magic so compelling it sweeps away all rational thought.

Moaning softly, Eva's tongue seeks entry into my mouth. The hard, powerful frame behind me rocks into mine from behind. Lean hips cradle my ass, a thickening length sandwiched between us. As the heat of illness breaks, I'm overwhelmed with these other sensual sensations.

I weave my fingers into the length of Eva's hair and kiss her deeply. She tastes of papaya and of the ocean I miss so badly. Hand winding around my neck, she draws me closer. With each passing minute, my vigor returns through Apollo's healing energy. It flares, building with every intimate exchange.

Lips find the nape of my neck. Firm and insistent, they scatter kisses to my shoulder. Apollo doesn't stop there. The hand resting on my hip begins to caress, swirling patterns over my skin.

Breathing rapidly, Eva takes my hand, placing it on the curve of her perfect breast. Her makeshift dress out of a bedsheet does little to hide her nakedness. Cheeks flushed, eyes sparkling with lust, she watches Apollo's hand drift down to encircle my cock. We're slaves to the magic that has us in its thrall. Prisoners of a wanton need.

Teasing the peak of her nipple into excitement, I dip my head to bathe it with my tongue. Eva mewls, head falling back on the pillows. Straining against me, she's desperate for the pleasure. The confident hand around my cock pumps up and down my length. Apollo knows just how to touch me. Teeth nip at my shoulder. Moaning, bucking my hips into his palm, my hand moves down between Eva's legs to her waiting wetness.

"Yes, touch her," Apollo urges, his voice low and raspy with arousal. "I want you to make her come. Just like I'm going to make you."

APOLLO
Chapter Ten

I can't fight it.

Seductive and enslaving magic thrums around the room. A decadent trap of lust and desire. The whole building vibrates with it. My curiosity as to how Pluto has kept his breeding camp successful has been answered. It's just another manipulation. Free will isn't a factor.

Now beautifully naked, Eva cries out as she twists on the mattress while Fontus toys with her clit. Her long brown hair a mess of silky waves over the pillows. He's just as lovely as she is. Muscled, tanned skin with attractive features. The contrast between feminine and masculine has my magic induced craving for them spilling out of control.

I need release.

Whether it's a tight pussy, a snug ass, or a warm, welcoming mouth is beside the point. All I know is this urge won't end until I come.

"Eva, wrap you lips around my cock." I order, still jerking off her lover with merciless strokes. Long and thick, his length has been a pleasing discovery.

She obeys without a word. Somehow, we all move at once, attuned to our joint need for completion. She helps me strip out of my shorts, and I abandon them on the floor.

Cock hard and bobbing free, it points eagerly toward her. Eva's pouty lips find the crown as she laps at the pre-cum. Engulfing it with her mouth, she takes my shaft down her throat, gagging prettily when she reaches her limit. Tangling my fingers in the locks of her hair, I direct her movements to the pace I need.

Eva spreads her thighs wide, and Fontus scoots between them. Mouth swooping down to her pussy, he continues what his fingers had started. Eva's pleasured groan vibrates through my length, causing it to swell harder with excitement. Playing with her lover, I feel him pulse within my grip. Writhing, pleasuring each other—we're delirious in erotic carnal passion.

Crying out, Fontus bathes Eva's tits with a jet of cum. It's a beautiful sight. Thighs trembling and tensing, she finds her own orgasm, her moan muffled as I fuck her face. I can't hold back. Three more short thrusts, and my cum shoots down her throat.

Releasing my hold on her hair, I fall back against the pillows. Panting, shaking, we all lay staring at each other while the insidious magic dissipates as quickly as it had appeared.

Breasts heaving, Eva's expression is of shock.

"What just happened?"

Fontus looks just as surprised and mortified beside her. Taking a corner of the sheet, he cleans his sticky cum from her naked body. The healing power I managed to muster has restored him to health, chasing away his fever.

"I'm guessing that's how Pluto encourages his captives to breed," I reply grimly.

"You mean it's some kind of enchantment to force us to have sex?"

Eva won't meet my eyes. A delicate shade of pink suffusing her cheekbones marks her embarrassment at what we've just taken part in. I should regret it, but I don't. The moment I'd seen her outside the building, I wanted a taste of her. Even without whatever was influencing us, I'm certain we would have ended up in bed together. If I have my way, once we're out of danger, we will again. Eva and Fontus make a beguiling pair. Perfectly matched.

I nod at her question. "Yes."

"We need to find a way off this Island," Fontus mutters, discarding the dirty sheet onto the floor. "If we've been caught up by that magic once, there's no saying when it might strike again. Your father knows where we are? If you don't check in he'll send others, right?"

"I didn't tell him the location of the island," I admit, palming the back of my neck with awkwardness. I'm an idiot. Selene had given me a warning. Instead of listening to her and alerting my father, I was cocky enough to think I could handle things alone.

Fontus' response is a long drawn out groan. "Please tell me your joking."

"Selene knows where we are." At their blank expressions, I elaborate further. "She's an oracle who gave me the location that led me here."

Sitting up, Eva grabs a ragged pillow and hugs it to her chest. "And you think she'll tell your father where we are?"

"Well...no. But I'm not the only one who goes to her. One of my brothers might seek her visions when I turn up missing."

"So, we have to sit here until someone realizes your missing?" She doesn't sound impressed.

We're still naked on the bed. The scent of sex lingers in

the air. I'm aware anyone could walk in on us at any time, including other occupants of the camp looking for fun. Sliding off the mattress, I go in search of my shorts.

"I never said that. It's a plan B. Right now we're going to get dressed, find you both something to wear, and scout the island. I want to know the source of the spell that's keeping this place shrouded," I respond, and having found my shorts, I pull them on and button them up.

EVA

My brain feels like it's going to explode. I can't believe what just happened with Apollo and Fontus. My cheeks still feel heated with the embarrassment of having Fontus' mouth on my pussy while I swallowed Apollo's dick. My blushes aren't from feeling it was wrong but from enjoying it. After everything I've been through the last few days with Pluto, I shouldn't want the attention of two men, but as we dress and leave the room to search for a way off the island, I feel safe in between them.

"We need to stay close to Eva." Fontus is behind me, his hand on the small of my back. "The men around here are crazy. We've already had to kill three of them."

"Is that how you got the injuries?" Apollo is in front of me. His massive hand dwarfing mine in its hold.

"Yes, one of the men was trying to attack her. We also made an escape and very nearly got to the water, but these strange creatures stopped us," Fontus explains, and I look between them, both men much taller than me.

"The island is magical. There are creatures here I've never seen before. All the fruits and vegetables grow in abundance. It's as though the island is hidden away from everyone, so the inhabitants can just breed for Pluto," I add.

Apollo frowns.

"It is concealed. I didn't know it was here until I hit it, basically."

"So as a god, even you couldn't see it from the outside?" Fontus stops, and we halt as well.

We're out in the garden now, the hot sun beating down on us. My dry skin longs for the rush of salty water over it.

"No, I couldn't. That mixed with my suppressed powers is worrying me more than anything. How long has Pluto had these camps and been breeding his army? How the hell didn't my father or any of the other gods know?"

We all fall silent, the burden of what we've discovered weighing heavily on us. If this has been happening for years, then Pluto could already have enough demigods to take over the world. I wrap my hand around my necklace. Its watery symbolism gives me strength as we follow Apollo back to the place on the island where he was able to land. I'm surprised Pluto doesn't know of its existence.

It doesn't take long to get down to the sea. This section of beach is tucked away from the view of the rest of the island, and none of the bird-like creatures descend on us. It's a forgotten part and the reason Apollo was able to come ashore without being noticed.

"I'm afraid I'm not as good a swimmer as you two are. You'll need to help me. My boat got somewhat destroyed when I hit the island." Apollo picks up a piece of wood from what must have once been his boat.

"I'm sure we can do that." Fontus leads me down nearer to the sea. "You ready?"

The scent of the ocean invades my nostrils, and I can feel my strength growing. The power of the waves re-invigorates my every pour. Shutting my eyes, I call to the sea, and my father's abilities that have been suppressed surge back into my body. Holding my hands out in front of me, I summon the water, and it rises up to meet my fingertips. It's warm and welcoming, but I don't dive in. Looking to my left, I see the same expression on Fontus' face that I must be wearing on my own. Bliss.

I turn to Apollo, but he's not watching us. His head is turned back toward the heart of the island. I can instantly tell he's worried about what is happening here. What the island means for the future of the gods. I hush the water's rejoicing and allow it to drop back down to its natural flow. Fontus looks at me.

"What are you doing?"

I kneel down before the water and dip a finger into it.

"Go on the wave, tell my father where we are. Get him to send a message to Jupiter."

"Eva?" Fontus questions with a lick of anger in his tone.

"I can't leave," I tell him while standing back up.

"You are getting the fuck off this island before anything else happens to you. I'll die before I let Pluto touch you again," Fontus demands.

Apollo must hear our conversation for he snaps out of his reflection on the island.

"What are you talking about, Eva?"

"We need to stay here." I look back to the jungle and where I know the house stands. "The water will let people know where we are, and they will come with their own army. But for now, we need to find out what Pluto's overall plans are. How many camps he has? Where the babies who've already been born are taken? We need to learn his plans, so we can put a stop to them. It's the only way."

"That's a dangerous thing to do," Apollo responds.

"I know, but as you said to me when you first saw me, I'm a silly little girl. I've done nothing but live off my father's reputation. It's time to change all of that and be the demigoddess I was born to be."

I have Pluto to thank for my change of heart. He didn't break me in the way he thought he would when he took me against my will. No, he helped me to grow up, and now I won't stop until I prevent him from doing what he did to others. Magic and mystery is at work on this island, but between Apollo, Fontus, and me, we have powers too. We'll bring an end to the breeding camps forever.

"Fontus?" Apollo pulls me to him. There's no question that Jupiter's son will also be staying on the island even with subdued powers. It's his job to keep the existence of the gods hidden from the world. "Are you staying or going?"

I don't expect Fontus to stay with me. He's been gone from the sea for so much longer than I have. He's suffered more than I have.

"Go," I urge him.

He shakes his head.

"Not without you. We're in this together until the very end."

FONTUS

Chapter Twelve

I know part of me should question Eva's decision to remain on the island and worry that something has happened to her sanity, but I understand her reasons for staying. They're the same as mine. To put a stop to Pluto and his scheme to breed his own army of gods for the Underworld.

We walk back to the house in silence. Eva collects another couple of papayas from a tree. I don't have the heart to tell her that their ability to prevent pregnancy is more of an old wives' tale than fact. If it's already happened, there's nothing we can do. But if it hasn't, at least Apollo and I will be able to protect her from it occurring with any of the other men on the island.

Our room is bathed in the evening sunlight when we return to it. The large bed welcomes me into its comfort when I collapse down on it. I'm still a little weary from my fever, but I'm healing well.

"I'll go and see if I can find another empty room for me to stay in." Apollo stands awkwardly at the door. The memory of his strong hand wrapped around my dick resurfaces, and I feel myself getting hard at the thought.

"No." The word leaves my lips before I have a chance to understand what I'm saying. Trying to backtrack quickly, I add, "It's safer for Eva if we all stay in here together. If one of us can't be here to protect her, then at least the other one is."

Eva slides next to me on the bed and rests her head on my chest.

"Thank you," she purrs.

"Are you sure?" Apollo asks and takes a seat on a rocking chair at the window. The sun's rays illuminating his blond curls.

"We'll find out as much as we can about Pluto's schemes, but we need to keep Eva safe," I confirm.

Apollo nods.

"I'll need to keep hidden as much possible. If my uncle learns I'm here, it will put you both in danger."

"Agreed."

"What do we do first?" Eva sits up on the bed.

She looks weary, and I realize she's probably not slept properly for days.

"Tonight, we sleep. Tomorrow, we explore the island. Make notes of the guards. Numbers of people here. Look for women who've had children. Ask them what has happened to the babies. We find out as much as we can and get ready for when back-up arrives," Apollo tells us, and I'm grateful he has noticed Eva's exhaustion as well.

"There is a lady in the kitchen—she prepares all the food. I think she'll be good to talk to. I met her earlier, and I felt she was keeping things from me," Eva informs us as she slides from the bed.

"Good idea. You speak to her. Fontus, see what you can find out from some of the other men. They can't all be crazed from the need for sex. I'll see what I can find out about the island. I'll stick to the shadows, so I can't be seen." Apollo gives us our orders, and we both nod in agreement with them. I'm glad he's here with us. His dominant nature allows him to take control and assign tasks.

"I'm going to have a bath, if that's ok." Eva meanders over to the bathroom attached to our room. "I want to try something now that I have some of my powers back."

I'm intrigued to know what she means, so I follow her with Apollo hot on my heels, his own curiosity piqued.

Eva kneels down beside the bath and turns the tap on.

"Regular water. It's good to drink, but there's nothing like a salt water bath."

She places her hand in the middle of the running water.

"Are you doing what I think you're doing?" I question and place my hand in the bath water. I instantly feel the saltiness of it. "I'm coming in with you."

I remove my clothes quicker than Eva can and jump into the bath big enough for two, obviously another ploy by Pluto to encourage relationships between his *guests*.

"Hey, not fair," she protests with a sexy little pout on her face but at the same time removes her clothes and squeezes into the tub with me. The water cleanses our skin. We spend so much time in the sea that the absence of water lapping at our pores dries it out.

"This is bliss." Eva moans and slips down under the water.

I remember Apollo is here with us when I hear the low rumble of desire emanate from his throat. My dick hardens under the weight of his hooded stare. Eva resurfaces and must sense the sexual tension in the room, for she instantly looks between us both.

"Eva, I want to watch you ride Fontus. Are you all right to do that?" Apollo lowers his hands into his shorts and re-arranges himself, presumably to relieve the pressure in his suddenly tight looking pants.

I don't want to force Eva into anything she's not ready for, but the sparkle in her eyes tells me she wants this as much as I do. She rises out of the water, like a goddess emerging from the sea, and positions herself over my hard cock. I stroke it a few times, and then she lowers her encapsulating warmth over me, sheathing me fully to the hilt.

"Fuck!" Apollo exclaims and lowers his shorts. His long length stands proud. He prowls toward us for a better view, holding his dick in his hand the entire time and squeezing it tightly. I can't stop watching.

Eva rises up from the water again, and I turn my attention back to her.

"Beautiful," I tell her, taking her left breast in my hand and caressing it. Apollo uses his free hand to tease at her right nipple.

"Stunning," he says.

"Full," Eva breathlessly mouths, her body now raising and lowering over my cock at a steady pace. The magical need for sex fills the room again. Sensibilities forgotten as Apollo strokes himself, and I assist Eva by burying my dick deep within her. Eva leans over toward Apollo and locks lips with him, their tongues dancing together in a passionate tango.

Our movements become more urgent, and my need to get as far inside her as I can more pressing.

"So good." Eva parts from Apollo. "Not salty … earthy. Different."

She kisses me next, and I can taste Apollo's earthiness on her lips.

He stops stroking himself and pulls our mouths apart. He forces a dominating kiss onto my lips, and I melt under his power. He's different to everything I've known before, and it excites me. I don't understand it, but I know that even though the magic controls our desires this need between the three of us is natural.

Eva whimpers her impending release, and Apollo takes his cock back in hand and strokes harder. My own orgasm shoots from my balls as Eva sinks down onto me one final time. The water of the bath sloshes over the side while her pussy pulsates around my dick and milks the cum from within me. All I can see is a fireball of stars. My head's spinning so much I'm only vaguely aware of Apollo pushing our heads together and covering our faces with his own release.

The magical spell breaks its cocoon around us, and guilt develops in my gut.

What are we doing?

How can we stop this?

Eva pushes herself off me, her cheeks reddened again.

Apollo is the only one who seems calm. He reaches out and draws a line through the cum on both our faces.

"We can't stop this spell on us. We made our decision to stay. Whatever happens on the island will stay here if that's what you want?" he tries to reassure us.

Tears fill Eva's eyes, and one drips into the bath water. It turns instantly cold around me.

I feel and see her sadness. It matches my own.

We are no longer in control of our own destinies.

Our decision to give ourselves over to the fight by remaining on the island might leave us all spiraling out of control, and Eva ... pregnant.

APOLLO
Chapter Thirteen

Stepping from the bathroom, my gaze travels over the length of the bed and the two figures sound asleep on the mattress. Fontus is spooning Eva, his brawny body protecting hers after the sadness of her tears last night. It had pulled at something deep inside my chest. They'd both been exhausted and needed sleep.

The desire to feel Eva's snug pussy or Fontus' ass squeezing my cock like a vice is hard to ignore. I'm not sure whether it's entirely the influence of this place. Last night, I was a slave to my desires. I'm certain that next time we're overcome with whatever inhabits these walls, I'll end up fucking one of them or both.

The little princess is stubborn. Remaining here will only lead her to become ripe with a child in her belly. Although I want her with a burning need, I know I can't allow it to be mine. She and Fontus are lovers. If things had progressed naturally, I'm more than sure they'd have ended up together anyway. If her fate is to bear a child, it is better that it's his.

Yet I can't erase the memory of how beautiful they'd both looked with my cum painted over their faces.

Dark and light.

My ebony and Ivory.

Cock semi-hard at the thought, I walk silently across the room, patting myself dry with a towel. The early morning shower was enough to rid myself of any lingering sleep. Refreshing after the heat of the hot tropical night and their tempting bodies pressed so intimately against my own.

The island must be scouted. I need to know the full extent of what we're up against and the layout of the land. Not having my powers is a nuisance. I've never been without them before, and it's left me feeling vulnerable, something a god like me should never experience.

We're all incredibly powerful.

Immortal.

Even if I do run into trouble, though, I'll have no problem defending myself. Sparring and training with my brothers for battle has molded me into a seasoned warrior.

Hopefully Eva and Fontus won't be bothered by the others residing in the house while I'm gone. When they wake, they'll be annoyed I've left them behind, but I'm more than aware they need to rest. I don't want them in any more danger. They've both been through enough and need to regain their strength for what's to come.

Finding my shorts, I stab my legs into them and pull them up my muscled thighs. Walking barefoot through a jungle isn't appealing—my lack of footwear won't get me very far. As I button up my shorts, I spy some scuffed, well-worn trainers under a tatty table in the corner of the room. Discarded and on the verge of falling apart, it looks like their owner abandoned them. Kneeling down, I drag them out. Stuffing my feet into them, they fit, which is a relief.

My eyes bounce back to the occupants of the bed. They look so peaceful together. The dawn sunlight slowly creeps over the mattress—its warm glowing rays already washing over their entwined legs.

Lovers come and go. I've never done permanency. That's just not me. Never been me. I tumble from one bed to another without a twinge of guilt at the broken hearts I leave behind. I shouldn't be experiencing this possessiveness. A sense that they're both mine.

After what happened in the bathroom, I think it's for the best I put some distance between us today. The magic of the island is far too strong, even for me. Hopefully they'll start questioning some of the other residents while I'm away.

Moving stealthily to the door, I slip out without a sound, and making sure it's closed properly behind me, I hurry down the corridor. I need to be gone before they awaken. There's no telling how many miles I have to cover to find the measure of the land.

Soft muffled moans and groans emanate from behind closed doors. Magic washes over my skin, sending goose-bumps in its wake. Whatever Pluto is doing, it's making his plan to breed soldiers successful. How long has he had this little operation running? Where are the offspring?

I frown at that nagging thought.

Unseen, I descend the stairs. It looks like everyone else rises later. Not surprising when all they do all day is fuck. The air is still cool as I step out of the front door, yet already there's a hint of the coming heat of the day. Striding purposefully toward the tree line, I keep my wits about me.

Reaching the end of the long, knee high grass that brushes my bare legs, I pause. Shading my eyes from the brightness of the sun with my hand, I spare a quick glance back at the house. My gaze lingers on the window at the top.

Their window.

I'll return for them.

That certainty is sure and strong in my soul.

Stepping into the trees, frightened birds screech, startled by my presence. The sound of their movement comes from high above, but I don't see them through the thick lushness of the vibrant green leaves. Moving inland is the most logical plan. The coast can be searched another day. Traversing the thick brown roots sticking up from the earth, I head west.

EVA

Chapter Fourteen

I can sense Apollo has left us before I even open my eyes. His domineering presence fills the room with a feeling of safety when he's here. The sounds of love-making filter up through the wooden floorboards of our room and bring bile to my throat. The spell Pluto weaves is incredibly powerful.

Rolling away from Fontus, he continues sleeping, I lay on my back and place my hand on my stomach. I'm not ashamed to admit I've been a spoiled brat most of my life. One of father's favorite children, I've never wanted for anything, but now it's time for me to grow up. The sea has healed my powers. With Apollo's abilities bound and Fontus' less than mine, I'm the most powerful of us all, at the moment. I need to use that power to ensure we find out everything we can about what's happening here, and I know just who to speak to first.

Climbing from the bed, I press a soft kiss to Fontus' head. He stirs, and sleepy green eyes look up at me.

"What are you doing?" his voice is husky from sleep .

"I'm going to get us some breakfast," I tell him as I pull on the sheet I've fashioned into a dress. Fontus folds back the bedcovers and stumbles out of the bed, looking for his tatty shorts. "No." I place my hand on his toned thigh. "Rest."

"Not happening, Eva. There's no way you're wandering around on your own."

Fontus' eyes roll. I can tell he's feeling dizzy, and reaching out to him, I help him sit back on the bed.

"I'll be fine, Fontus. You're still recovering and need to rest." I place a hand on my hip and stare him down.

"I need to protect you." Fontus tries to stand again, but I'm quicker.

There is a glass of water by the side of the bed. I swirl my hand and form a pair of cuffs with the clear liquid. One cuff wraps around his wrists and pulls him back onto the bed while the other cuff fixes itself to the bedpost, keeping him in place.

"Eva. Take them off," he growls at me in annoyance.

"Do you agree to rest?" I question with a raised eyebrow.

"It's too risky. I can't let you walk around unprotected." He looks around the room. "Where's Apollo?"

I shrug my shoulders.

"Gone."

"Abandoned us?" he questions.

"I don't know. I hope he sends reinforcements if he has."

A strange warmth floods through my body. It's mysterious in nature, but it tells me that Apollo is still on the island. Fontus stops struggling against the water cuffs as if he's just been hit by the same sensation.

"He's still here," Fontus confirms. His breath labored with the thick lust swirling in the room.

"I know." I wave my hand and the water cuffs disappear. "You'll know if I need you," I tell him. It's the magic surrounding us, weaving us closer together so we're almost one.

Fontus looks down at the bed. He's deep in thought for a

few moments before looking back up at me with a beautiful, big smile on his face. "I will know. I'll rest for an hour more, and then I'll start questioning a few people."

I lean over him as he settles back into the bed and press a longing kiss to his lips. I know if I don't leave the room now, the spell on us will have me fucking him for the rest of the day, and Apollo when he returns. I make sure the makeshift sheet dress covers as much of my body as possible and tiptoe into the corridor and down to the kitchen.

The elderly lady I met before stands at the stove cooking what looks like bacon and eggs. She mixes the hearty breakfast together over a flame that dances in the cool breeze of the early morning coming in through the open door.

"Breakfast is in the dining room. If you want anything special, let me know." She looks up at me with a smile, and I return it.

My stomach rumbles, suddenly feeling very hungry at the delectable smells filling the kitchen.

"Some of that would be nice, if that's ok?" I ask and pick up a plate from the large stack on the counter next to her. "Do you need any help?"

She shakes her head.

"This is my job. You should be with that man of yours." She looks down to my stomach. "I meant it when I said getting pregnant will make you safer."

I place my hand on my flat stomach as the lady places some of the bacon and eggs onto my plate.

"Knowing more about the island will keep me even safer, and I think you're the person who can tell me what I need to know." I take a seat at the counter and pick up a fork. Spearing a piece of bacon and egg with it, I take a bite. It's delicious, the best food I've ever tasted, and being a demigoddess, I've eaten in many places around the world.

"You're wrong. I can't tell you anything." The lady places the rest of the food onto the plate and disappears out of the kitchen door. It's one of those that flips backward and forward until it settles on its hinges.

I take another couple of mouthfuls while I wait for her to return. I don't have to wait long. She re-appears with an armful of dirty plates and begins to wash them up with her back to me.

"Eva," I tell her. She doesn't turn to face me. "That's my name. What's yours?"

"Nothing important," she replies still feverishly scrubbing the dishes to get them clean.

"It's important to me."

She puts down the dish she's holding and bows her head.

"Go back to your man. Don't do this. It will only lead to trouble."

"How do you know?"

I hear a sob come from her and get to my feet. But then stop when she starts to lift the back of her top. The suntanned flesh of her back is marred with silvery scars that can only come from the tail of a whip.

"This is how I know." She lowers her top and turns to face me, her eyes red at the rim. "You've so much of myself in you. Heart and spirit. A love of the sea. Don't fight this—it'll break you in ways that you can never imagine."

"You're a water goddess."

"I was a demigoddess. Have you heard of The Lady of the Lake?"

"Isn't that Arthurian legend?" I try to remember my

schooling, but I didn't pay a lot of attention in history. It wasn't my subject.

"It was based around me, but the story was skewed over the years. My father was a Roman god, my mother his Celtic lover. I lived in a spring near Hadrian's wall until I was captured by Pluto. My name is Coventina."

The name rings bells in my head, but all I remember is her disappearing a thousand or so years ago.

"How long have you been here?" I ask, fearing the answer.

"Too long. I was the first breeder. This place is my home now. I don't even know if my spring still exists."

"You were the first breeder?"

"I gave Pluto his first child for his army. I lost count of how many he took from me after that. Endless, until I was too old. He was surprisingly sentimental about me being his first, and he allowed me to remain here unlike the many others he killed."

The bacon and eggs suddenly stick in the back of my throat. I can't eat any more. I think I'll bring it all back up if I do.

"Can you tell me about this army?"

"On the other side of the island. That's where he keeps them until they are old enough to go into battle for him. There weren't many at first, but now there are so many of you here, and in the other camps as well. I fear it won't be long before he has enough to take over the Earth. He hates the inhabitants of the land above him. They bow down to Jupiter and not him. He will see them all destroyed for that betrayal."

"Why did you stay? You could have used the water to escape?" I push away from the counter, and coming closer to her, I wrap my arms around her. She leans her head against my shoulder, and I feel the wetness of her tears soak into the sheet.

"I put my foot in the sea once. I felt my body slipping away with the current. I allowed it to take my powers for another to use. I knew, as you do now, that this needed to be stopped. The problem was I didn't have the two men you have by your side. I was alone."

"T-two men?" I stutter. Apollo needs to be hidden from sight. His presence if discovered would lead him into trouble. "I only have Fontus."

Coventina pulls back from where she's shed her tears and runs a hand down my face.

"No, my darling. I sense the truth. You have a weapon that could destroy Pluto if used in the right way. Apollo does have the ability to wield his powers—he just doesn't know it yet."

FONTUS

Chapter Fifteen

Tossing restlessly on the bed, I throw an arm over my eyes to keep out the light streaming in through the window. Eva's been gone for ages. The minutes have ticked by endlessly, and my worry only rises.

I should have gone with her.

None of us should be alone in this place.

It's not safe for any of us here. I wish Apollo had taken us with him. Whatever peril awaits us on the rest of the island, we should face it together.

Releasing a sigh, I rise from the bed, bare feet slapping against the wooden floor. I may not be at full capacity, as Eva pointed out, but I can still fight.

I head for the bathroom and quickly wash before putting on my previously discarded shorts. The sounds of sex and pleasure emanate from the walls. It appears the other occupants are awake.

I still don't understand why they haven't tried to escape or at least try to leave this house. All the magic induced fucking. Is this what they want? To be Pluto's puppets? Their children ripped from their arms to be used to destroy the world?

I imagine Eva pregnant. A small innocent babe cradled in

her arms. She could have conceived already. She could be carrying my child.

Gripping the sides of the white porcelain sink, a pair of green eyes stare back from the mirror in front of me. Instead of feeling anxiety at the prospect I might be a father, all I can wonder is whether the baby will have the same color as me? I've never imagined myself as a dad. Being immortal, I have all the time in the world. Yet I know that if Eva is pregnant, I will protect her and our offspring until my last breath.

The sound of the bedroom door opening drags me from my thoughts. Smiling at my reflection in relief, I hurry back to greet her.

My feet stop dead in the doorway when I realize it's not Eva. A tall gaunt stranger is standing in middle of our room. A mane of white hair flows down his shoulders, bright in contrast with the black he's dressed head to toe in. Just behind him are four large males, who remind me of night-club bouncers. Muscled, mean looking with steely, determined expressions.

"Who are you?" I ask, dread curling around my heart.

Tilting his head in my direction, the stranger's gaze bores into mine, icy and remote. "My name is Ambrose. You will refer to me as Principal Ambrose. I govern this island and everyone on it for Pluto. Where's the female you are with?"

"She went for a walk." It's not completely a lie. I know Eva is questioning others, but instinct tells me that if Ambrose finds that out, it will be dangerous for her.

Turning, he addresses two of the guards. "Find her. Bring her to me."

Both bow their heads in response before leaving.

Ambrose returns to his observation of me. It makes my skin crawl the way he stares at me. Being the center of this man's attention is a very bad thing—I'm not certain how I know, but I do.

"Now you've had time to settle in, I'm here to check both of you over and make sure you are indeed healthy and able to procreate," he tells me tonelessly with just a hint of disgust.

Edging farther back into the room, I put the bed between us.

"What do you mean by check?"

Clicking his fingers, one of the men behind him, carrying a black leather bag, hurries to a rickety wooden table. The fact it looks like a doctor's case is the first thing I notice.

Ambrose watches me unblinking, drinking in my reaction as it's snapped open and the contents are laid out.

Metal gleams in the sunlight, clamps, retractors, forceps and other things I know are used to be inserted to examine women internally. Two syringes are among the items together with empty vials for taking blood and clear sterile pots.

My mouth goes dry as the guard hands Ambrose a pair of blue latex gloves.

"I require a sample of your blood and a specimen of your semen," he informs me, snapping the gloves on and working them down his long skinny fingers. "It's better that you don't resist me."

Panic makes my chest tight and breathing rapid. I'm not about to give either of them up voluntarily. I've got to warn Eva. Get her out of here and into the jungle where, if we're lucky, they won't be able to find us.

For the first time since he entered the room, an emotion glimmers in Ambrose's eyes. Dark amusement. "You're not the first on the island, and you won't be the last to try and defy me. I always get what I want, boy. There's no escape from this place so give up any notions of playing hero. Here you are nothing but filthy animals sent to breed. If you disobey the rules, you will not enjoy the results."

"No." I shake my head, grasping onto my courage. "I'm not going to give you what you want."

Ambrose's lips stretch in a twisted smile. "I thought you might say that. Hold him down."

The hulking guards come at me as one. Nimbly I leap across the mattress, evading one as he makes a grab at me. Their master is blocking the exit. Grabbing a chair, I slam it into the second guard, and the wooden frame shatters against his body. It stuns him enough for me to make a run for the bathroom. The door looks solid enough to keep them out. If I can block it with something, I can chance escaping through the window. Being on the top floor, the drop is high, but I know it won't kill me. Suddenly, searing pain erupts through my veins—a burning spark sets my body alight in a chain reaction. It sends me smashing to the floor beside the bathtub. The agony is so intense for a moment I think I might pass out as colored blotches dance in front of my eyes, blinding me.

"Do you feel my power? Yours may be bound here, but mine are not. I can rip your insides apart without even laying a hand on you." Ambrose's mouth is close to my ear, his sickly sweet breath causing the hairs on the back of my neck to creep up. "Such sweet suffering."

Bony, gloved fingertips shimmer across my cheek as a whimper slips from my throat. Now I understand. He's the reason everyone stays compliant. He's the monster heading this camp and ensuring it's successfulness. Twitching in pain, my limbs feel heavy, and I'm unable to move them as my sight returns. The first thing I see is Ambrose's sinister face above me.

"Keep a hold of him," he instructs his guards, holding up a syringe. "I don't want to waste a drop."

Rough hands grab my shoulders and legs, keeping me pinned down. I hiss at the sting shooting up my arm. Darting a peek, I see my blood being drawn up into the little vial.

"If you aren't a suitable match for the sea goddess you've paired yourself with, then we'll find you both new play-mates," he tells me.

No. I can't let them separate us. Where the hell is Apollo? Please, please let Eva be safe. I know how stubborn she can be. I don't want her to put herself at risk for me.

"Remove his shorts."

The cold command has me struggling with growing desperation as my shorts are shoved down my legs. With no other clothes on, I'm now naked and at their mercy.

Ambrose stares down at my cock with a raised eyebrow. When his latex covered fingers encircle my flaccid member, I flinch.

"Now be a good boy and come for me," he encourages, slowly working my length up and down.

There's no way that's going to happen. His touch fills me with disgust and loathing. The guards still have me held in place, their weight keeping me trapped on the wooden floor —its coolness spreads up my spine. It's then I feel the wisp of magic. It coils upward from beneath me, wrapping itself around my body. Eyes widening in shock, my cock hardens, surging into life with a will of its own.

"No!" The word is torn from me in a raw cry. I suddenly have no control over my body. Realization that I'm trapped in the spell that shrouds this place sends bile rising in my throat.

"That's it. Feel the pleasure ... give into it." Ambrose's voice is thick with lust as he jerks me off faster. "I can't wait to examine your pretty little friend, and when I'm done, I think I'm going to fuck her. It's always fun to break the feisty ones. They're never that way for long. I'll strip her of her fight and turn her into one of our top breeders."

Crying out in confusion, my hips thrust up, demanding more. The need to come is a primal urge. Images flood my head. Eva strapped to an examination table while Ambrose forces himself on her. Other men taking her over and over, covering her with their cum. Instead of feeling abhorrence at the scene, it sends my excitement spiraling. With a harsh groan, I cum all over my captor's gloved hand as well as decorating my stomach in white pearly ribbons.

Slumping in defeat, I keep my eyes closed. The sick, warped enchantment was playing with my mind. I know that, but it doesn't stop me from experiencing terrible shame and guilt.

APOLLO

Chapter Sixteen

Wiping sweat from my face with the palm of my hand, I lick my dry lips. I'm not sure what time it is. Somewhere above, the sun is hidden by a canopy of branches and vibrant green leaves. The jungle is alive with wildlife. Fruits of all description hang in abundance, including some that shouldn't be able to survive in this climate.

This island is an enigma.

Its origins are a mystery, and I keep questioning how it can even exist. Why have we never known about it? After centuries of living on this planet, why has it never been discovered? How long has Pluto kept it a guarded secret? What else does he have we don't know about?

These thoughts send a chill through me. Sinking down onto a sturdy, fallen tree trunk, I take a moment to gather my bearings. I've been walking for miles. The trees seem to stretch endlessly with no sign of a break. How big can this place be?

I need to turn back soon. A sense of foreboding has been churning in my gut, but I've been choosing to ignore it.

Eva and Fontus.

Somehow I know it's linked to them. Even with this distance between us, I haven't been able to shake the certainty that they're both mine. It's deep in my bones. A knowledge that's kept me worrying about them every second we've been apart. It scares the hell out of me. I don't understand what it means or if it could even work between the three of us.

Pushing myself up onto my feet, I tread forward. Just a little bit farther, and then I'll return to them. Next time I venture out, they'll be at my side.

One second, I'm surrounded by trees, and the next, I'm standing on a rolling hill. It dips down into a rocky valley. Encircling either side are breathtaking mountains capped with snow. Blinking in astonishment, I take in the scene. Beyond I see azure water glistening far in the distance and a stretch of green grassland.

An enchantment?

Glancing over my shoulder, I find the beginning of the tree line. Someone's deliberately woven a mirage to hide half of the island away, but why?

Frowning, I scan the view for any signs of life. A herd of white horses graze in the long swaying grass. Birds swoop and dive overhead. All looks serene and peaceful.

There has to be a reason. Why go to so much trouble?

Torn between forging on and the lovers I've left behind, my heart wins over my head. Tomorrow, we'll retrace my steps and investigate together, bringing water and all the provisions we need. The farther we're away from the house the better. Maybe we'll be safe from the sex inducing magic out here among nature.

Decision made, I head back into the trees. I'm once more in a dense, endless jungle. Quickening my steps, my pace sure, I hurry back in the direction of the house. There's no time to rest until I'm once more in their presence. I have some explaining to do. Eva will be annoyed I left them, and so will Fontus. Hopefully what I have to tell them will go some way to taming their anger. That and being able to touch them again. Anticipation at what tonight will bring between us makes me smile.

EVA

"Coventina, please, you can't tell anyone that Apollo is here. If Pluto finds out, it will be dangerous for him." I beg the older woman, my hands clasped together in a prayer.

"You don't have to worry, child. Pluto will not find out from my lips. I don't owe him anything. It's this island that's my home, not the person who brought me here." Coventina smiles at me, and I warm with the sense of maternal love emanating from her. I pick up a tea towel and start to dry the dishes. "You don't have to do that."

"I want to." I look around for where the dish goes. She points at a cupboard, and I put it away. "You said you had children taken from you, and they're on the other side of the island?"

"Yes." Coventina hands me another washed dish.

"How many do you think have been taken from you and the others over the years?"

"Hundreds. They are powerful children, the offspring of demigods and goddesses. They are trained from birth to fight. They don't know any differently." Coventina looks forlornly into the soap suds of the sink. "I went to see one of my children. He was little more than eight but already dressed for battle. He wasn't a boy any longer—his eyes were dead."

I go quiet, worried for my newfound friend's offspring. It's no way to be brought up. I don't want a child born from my body to have to experience that.

"Is it difficult to get to the other side of the island?" I question.

"If you are one of Pluto's people, then no. It's designed to keep us away. Our job is not to care for our children. It's to produce more." She leans down and opens a cupboard. Inside is a tub containing a blue concoction of some sort. "Magic makes you procreate. It doesn't make you forget though— that is the hardest part. Birth after birth, child after child all taken away. Pregnancy and then nothing to hold at the end. It damages you. This potion helps."

"Pluto gave you this?" I take the tub and examine it. It seems to be a natural mixture of herbs and flowers. Fontus would know more about it with his knowledge of mystical medicines. "I don't understand why Pluto wouldn't just use magic to make you forget."

"Because he's a man and doesn't have maternal instincts. It's natural for a mother who's carried a child to feel its loss. He didn't give me this medicine—I made it myself. Memories of magical spells embedded in my head from my Celtic side gave me the ability. I place a little in all the food I cook. It helps those here from suffering as I did." A tear tumbles down her cheek.

"But you don't take it yourself."

"I did at first, but I no longer want to forget."

I feel my own eyes well with tears. My heart breaking for all this gracious and kind woman has suffered. A noise outside the door draws our attention away from our solemn reflection.

"Where is she?" A deep voice asks as plates crash, and a woman screams.

"We don't know. We've not seen her," another male voice responds.

"If I find out you're lying, you'll be flogged."

"We're not. I promise," a female voice desperately pleads her case.

"Eva," the deep voice calls out, and I freeze. Coventina grabs the tub from me and places it back in the cupboard. "It's time for your examination. Come out."

"Examination?" I whisper to my friend. She turns pale.

"You need to hide." She looks around the room.

"Coventina, why does that man want me?" I'm nervous. I don't understand what is happening. Who are these men, seeking me out?

"When you first come here, the principal, a man named Ambrose, carries out tests on you. Checking your blood and fertility—he's not gentle or kind. If you think what Pluto has done to you is bad, then Ambrose is far worse. Can you curl up small?"

I gulp. "Yes, and I can do this ..." I place my finger into the washing up water, and it covers my body turning it to liquid and drawing it into the sink. I'm hiding in plain sight and won't be seen. The water is dirty and bits of discarded food cover me, but it doesn't bother me—I can see and hear everything.

The kitchen door slams open, and two burly men enter. The looks on their faces promise malevolence if they find me. I just have to hope they don't have magical abilities of their own and can see my spell. "Have you seen the new girl?"

Coventina crosses her arms over her chest.

"If you push that door any harder, it'll come off its hinges."

"Then you'll have to figure out how to put it back up, won't you? Or you could spread your legs and let me fuck that saggy pussy of yours to earn my help." One of the men comes over to my friend and places his face directly in front of her. "Where is she?" he spits the words at her.

"Just left. Fancied a walk in the gardens."

The man places his hand under Coventina's chin and grips it tightly. I know he's hurting her by the expression of pain on her face.

"You told her what delights were heading her way then?"

"I know not to break the rules." She shuts her eyes in subservience.

"Bullshit! I bet you told her how big my dick is, and she's scared." Both the men laugh evilly.

"I don't think she'll be impressed. She was telling me how big her partner is," Coventina retorts, and the man squeezes harder. She yelps in pain.

"What, the sniveling little whelp that Ambrose is currently getting sperm from? Yeah, I think his dick is probably shrunk inside at the moment. You know how good Ambrose is at getting what he wants." The other man simulates his insides being pulled apart. "Argh the pain!! No, please, take my cum."

The men laugh again, and I want to jump out of the water and run to Fontus. He's suffering again at the hands of these mad men, and I want nothing more than to protect him. Coventina moves her hand behind her back and dips it in the water. I wrap myself around her fingers to keep calm. I can't win against these men. I can't show my abilities to them. We have to play the long game, and that means hiding away, knowing Fontus is suffering.

"If your done being imbeciles, then I have people to cook for. As I said, she's in the garden."

The man holding Coventina brings his hand back and sends it flying into the older lady's face. She sways but doesn't fall.

"You'll pay for that rudeness later," he snarls in her face and releases her. He nods to the other guy. "Let's go. She's probably heading into the jungle to hide. We can play cat and mouse."

They both leave the room laughing. I wait a few moments before coming out of the water and turning back into my human form.

"Are you ok?" I check on my friend.

"I'm good. I promise," she replies, but when I inspect her cheek, I see it turning red.

"I swear I'll ..."

"No," Coventina interrupts my potent rage. "Go to your man. He'll need you now."

I take her hand and squeeze it.

"I *will* set you free from this." I turn to make my way back up to the bedroom, hoping I can avoid the guards and this Principal Ambrose. As I head out of the door, I swear I hear Coventina respond with ...

"Only death can do that."

FONTUS

Chapter Eighteen

Pulling myself up from the floor when Ambrose and his two guards leave, I stumble to the shower and turn the water to scalding. Climbing in, I allow the shame and guilt to be burned off my skin. I need to continue to be strong for Eva.

Shit!

Eva!

Turning the water off, I go to step out of the shower as she runs into the room.

"Fontus?" She slams her body into mine. "Are you ok?"

I try to tell her I'm fine. However, the words don't come out. I'm silent, my mouth opening and closing. I have to be strong for her, but I'm feeling the weight of the world on my shoulders at the moment. She turns the shower back on when I start to shiver. The water scalds her, and she jumps back to adjust the temperature.

"Did they find you?" I eventually manage to ask.

"I hid." She takes the soap and starts to wash me, her tiny hands dwarfed against my large body. She rubs away the dirt of shame and cleanses me in a way that only she can … with her pure kindness and love for me.

"We need to leave the island. It's too risky."

She shakes her head.

"We can't. There are children here." She looks up at me with her sorrowful eyes.

"What?"

"The children who are born here. They live on the other side of the island. We have to save them."

"Eva?"

"She's right." Apollo's deep voice comes from the doorway to the bathroom. "I know how to get there as well."

"We have to save them. Stop Pluto's plan, no matter what, Fontus." Eva leans her head against my chest and presses a soft kiss to the center of it.

Apollo strides across the room. He pulls the shirt off his head and lowers his shorts before stepping into the now cramped shower.

The sexual tension in the room crackles again, the magic wrapping itself around us.

"For now, though, we surrender," Eva says as she removes her sodden sheet dress and stands naked between us. My body tingles with need despite the orgasm ripped from me by Ambrose not long ago. Apollo stands behind me. Eva lowers to her knees in front of me. "We'll help you to forget,"

"In every way." Apollo runs his hands over the corded muscles of my back and down toward my buttocks. I lose myself in the feeling of their explorations.

Eva takes my hardening cock in her hand and flicks her tongue over the tip. I groan out my appreciation. She wraps her mouth around the length and draws it into her perfect mouth, causing memories of Ambrose's disgusting fingers touching it to dissipate. Apollo then lowers to his knees and pulls apart the mooned cheeks of my backside. I've never explored this sort of side of myself before, but it feels right in his hands. His finger circles at the bud of my hidden hole and tests the give there. I tighten involuntarily at the intrusion, but when Eva licks the entire length of my dick, I relax again, and Apollo is able to push a finger into my ass.

"Tight." He presses a kiss to my back. "Virgin. I'll lay claim to your virginity, Fontus."

"It's yours." I push back, allowing his finger deeper within my channel. Eva brings my dick farther into her mouth and gags. I fling my arms out and brace them against the wet wall to prevent myself from falling over.

"Fuck!" I exclaim as Apollo twists his finger inside me and rubs against a part of my body that has my legs quivering. I can't control myself. I've never felt anything like this before. I'm going to come quickly like a fucking schoolboy.

"Eva." I try to warn her but before I manage to I'm coming, coming, and coming into her mouth and throat. She swallows as much of it as she possibly can, but it drips out of her mouth and down her chin. I'm flying so fucking high that nobody could ever bring me down. Bad memories vanish, replaced with only this.

Apollo pulls his finger out and stands up. Eva moves aside and wipes her mouth as I bend and offer her my hand to help her to her feet.

"Hands back on the wall." Apollo orders me, and in my high state, I obey without thinking.

"Beautiful," Eva whispers as Apollo covers my body with his. His hard length nestling between the cheeks of my butt.

"This excites you, Eva?" Apollo teases and pushes his dick toward my entrance. "Watching me fuck Fontus, would that make you come?"

"Hell yes," she lowers her hand down her body, skimming

over the tight pebbles of her nipples and moving it toward the cleft between her thighs.

"Stop," Apollo orders, and she does before she's able to touch herself down there. "Should we allow her, Fontus? To stroke that pussy of hers and to dip her fingers inside herself while she watches my dick disappear inside your virgin asshole?"

"Please," Eva whimpers with thick need. "You two together are a work of art. I want to watch it forever."

"Nothing on this island is forever," I respond. "Nothing on this island is real. But in this moment, I want your fingers deep in your pussy, Eva, as you rub your clit and think about what Apollo is doing to me. And afterward, I want to watch him take you as well. We have this moment. Our moment, and then we fight or die ... maybe both"

As I finish my declaration, Apollo unceremoniously surges forward into my ass. It hurts like nothing I've ever experienced before. He's big, so fucking big, and it's tearing me apart, but I want him there. Every fucking inch. I'll want him always. Shit, the realization hits me like a ton of bricks. What the hell is the island doing to our minds as well as our bodies?

Apollo doesn't move—he allows me to adjust to him. Eva's eyes wide with desire watch us intently. Her fingers lower to her pussy, and she pulls apart the delicate petals of her sex to show us her clit emerging from beneath its protective covering. She strokes the length of her slit, up and down and back again, collecting her juices and the water of the still running shower before sinking two fingers inside herself. She moans, and Apollo's dick swells even more within me. He's a barrel of hardness embedded within my most private place. He withdraws to the tip, and I instantly lament the loss of him. I feel empty and weakened, but the second he pushes back into me, I feel complete.

"Damn, you feel so good. So tight around my dick. You're strangling it. I might never be able to pull all the way out again." Apollo breathes into the back of my neck, his teeth sinking into the delicate flesh of my collar bone. His calloused hands grip tightly to my hips, and he starts to use me as his fuck toy. With a woman, I always feel I have to be careful not to break them, but with a man, it's different because we're stronger.

"Good," I growl out through gritted teeth. "Stay there forever. Sod freedom let's just stay like this."

Apollo laughs behind me.

"That's the spell talking, not you."

Eva's still touching herself as her body slides down the wall, and she collapses onto the shower floor. We can see every intimate thing she's doing to herself—it's mesmerizing. Apollo grunts and propels his cock inside me. I'm losing control of my body. I feel like I'm flying outside of my skin. My hands remain pressed against the wall, stabilizing me while he enters me from behind. I watch my fingers and the way the water flows over them. It's not a natural motion, and sliding my left hand over the wall, the water follows.

"Fontus." Eva gasps. She continues to stroke herself with the tiny fingers of one hand, but when she lifts her other hand, the water surrounding it rises and circles in a pattern. I take one hand off the wall and the water comes with it, swirling around my wrist. I have my powers back! I'm not as magical as Eva, because she's the King's daughter, but I can control water.

Eva's head flops back, and she closes her eyes as she orgasms. Apollo buries himself deep inside me, and I feel the hot spurts of his cum warming my insides. It's like a dream I see and feel, but I'm not really there. I look down to my own dick, and I'm coming again, the white ribbons coating the shower wall in front of me. The magic on this island scares me, but it's drawing me into something I'm not sure I want to escape from.

APOLLO

Chapter Nineteen

The desire to fuck Eva here and now is strong, but I manage to resist as the magic ebbs. I'll have her soon, but right now with danger all around us, I have to think with my head not my dick.

Quickly washing myself clean, I direct them to do the same. Echoes of pleasure ring through me at the claiming of Fontus. He'd been so much better than I'd imagined. Spending time exploring his body as well as Eva's is something I intend to do when we are safe. If we're lucky, the lust spell woven around this section of the island doesn't extend far.

"What's the plan?" Fontus asks once he's pulled his ripped shorts back on. Eva is sitting on the edge of the mattress in her makeshift dress.

"The guards are still looking for Eva. We need to leave before they return from combing the jungle."

Fontus' dark eyes become wells of pain. "Ambrose had a bag of surgical instruments. What he did to me was bad, but what he plans for Eva is worse."

Ambrose, the man in charge. I'd overheard some of his goons talking when I'd slipped back to the house. The fact he wants to hurt my little sea goddess sends anger coursing through my veins.

Eva shudders where she's perched on the mattress, dainty arms hugging her body. Although she hides behind a shield of bravery, I can see the fine cracks already appearing. I need to keep her safe … both of them safe.

"Gather what you need," I order. "We're going into the jungle as far away from here as possible."

"Will it be far enough though?" Eva asks, her expression laced with worry. "They control all of it."

I understand her concerns. They've been my own, but I'm not about to voice them. We need all the positivity we can get right now. Striding across the room, I hunt though a pile of rags in a corner.

"What matters right now is getting away from this building. As I said before, I think I know where the children are being held. The other end of the island is very different from this side." Finding what's left of an old t-shirt, I take it, along with a frayed shoelace.

"What are you doing?" Fontus questions, his curiosity drawing him to my side.

Knotting the arm holes, I make sure nothing can escape. "This is a crude bag. Once we have placed what we need inside, we can tie it closed and use the shoelace as a handle."

Getting the idea, Eva quickly strips off a pillowcase. "How about this?"

I nod in approval. "We have plenty of fruit to eat when we're out there. What we need is drinkable water, a knife, matches to make a fire … and anything else practical we can carry."

"All that will be downstairs." Fontus points out, hurrying

to the window and scanning the world beyond. "We'll have to hurry."

Checking for danger, we exit the bedroom, sneak along the corridor, and descend the stairs. The atmosphere is strangely subdued. With Ambrose on the prowl, it looks like the rest of the occupants are staying clear of his path. Not that I blame them. I've not run into him yet, and I'm not looking forward to it when I do. He has got to be vile to be one of Pluto's favored enforcers. Cruel, sadistic, and brutal is usually the running criteria.

We hurry through the dining room. I grab some bottles of natural water and stuff them into my t-shirt bag. Eva copies me, throwing some into her worn out pillowcase. Meanwhile, Fontus is on point searching for any signs of our foes. As we move into the kitchen, an old woman looks up from where she's sitting by a table. A pile of potatoes is in front of her, and using the knife in her gnarled hand, she's peeling them one at a time. A red welt is fresh on her cheek.

"Eva?" she questions, eyeing us all suspiciously.

Reaching her side, the sea goddess drops to her knees. "Coventina, please you have to help us. We're going into the jungle, but we need to be prepared."

The old woman shakes her head of gray hair. "It's dangerous."

"I'll have Fontus and Apollo with me. We can't remain here any longer, not with Ambrose and his men searching for me."

A resigned sigh rises from Coventina's fragile chest. "You've taken some bottles of water from the other room?"

I nod when she glances up at me. I show her my stash before resting the makeshift bag on my shoulder and wrapping the shoe lace handle around my palm.

Getting to her feet with the help of Eva, Coventina shuffles around her kitchen, searching through drawers. "Matches, you'll need these."

When she tosses me the small box, I catch them with ease.

Tugging a sheathed knife from a cupboard, she places it in Eva's hand. "Don't lose this. You'll need it."

Unsheathing it carefully, Eva lets the sharp blade glint dangerously in the light. Although I didn't see any predators among the trees, it might be a different story at night.

Fontus gives us a look from the doorway where he's keeping watch, nervous energy spilling off him. I can sense his urgency that matches my own. We need to get moving as quickly as possible.

Coventina produces a flashlight, mirror, and a compass to go with the things we've already acquired. Eva takes responsibility for these, placing them into her pillowcase.

"Thank you, Coventina. We'll come back for you," she tells the older woman, planting a chaste kiss on her wrinkled cheeks.

Coventina's eyes glitter with tears. "You two look after her, you hear? Don't let anything bad happen to her, or you'll have me to deal with."

"I promise," I vow, noting the motherly way she watches Eva. "Keep your head down, Coventina, and just carry on like normal."

That causes her to huff. "Don't you go worrying about me. It's yourselves you have to be concerned about. They have things living on the island that only come out at night. Patrols. Not to mention the flock of winged beasts preventing us from reaching the sea." She fixes me with a stare. "I know where you're headed, and it's more dangerous than you think."

My gut clenches with the knowledge, but I keep the emotion from my face. "We have to try."

Wiping her damp eyes with her calloused fingers, she shoos us away with a cloth. "Go then! Before they find you."

Fontus opens the backdoor and strides out into the fresh air. As I go to join him, I see Eva hanging back, wearing a torn expression. I can see the bond between these two women is strong. If we were anywhere else, I would urge Coventina to come with us. But with the island's rough terrain, I know she'd only be a hindrance. This is the best place for her at the moment.

"Eva," I call softly.

Giving the old lady one last hug, Eva hurries to catch up, her now heavy pillowcase swinging from her shoulder.

"No," I tell Fontus as he steps in the direction I'd taken that morning. "The guards went that way. We'll go along the shoreline, not too close to the water, though. We don't need those flying monsters attacking. Then we'll cut back into the trees."

In silence, we head toward the beach, our pace hurried and hopes high.

EVA

I don't think I've ever been so relieved to get away from anywhere as I have the house we've been confined to since coming to the island. Its menacing features are behind us now, and the only thing I worry about is my friend Coventina. I'm comforted by the knowledge that we'll end this soon, though, and free her. We've got no option but to take the path we are now on. If there are children born here and enlisted into Pluto's army, then we need to free them.

"Be careful." Apollo grabs my hand to prevent me from slipping on the sharp rocky outcrops we've come across. Having left the jungle behind we've been traveling through fields and woodlands of green. The ice capped peaks looming in front of us are imposing at best. This island is a contradiction in terms. Both of the men have shoes on, but I'm barefoot. It's slowing us down, but we've little choice. I don't often wear shoes on the beach, so my feet are hardened to the ground, but if we have to go higher into the mountains to reach the other side of the island, then we are likely to encounter problems.

"Thank you," I offer Apollo.

"Do you think we should rest for a while?" Fontus looks down at me, worry etched on his face.

"No, I'm fine. A few more miles." I look up at the sky and see the oranges and reds of the sun setting. "We'll need to find somewhere to rest in a few hours anyway. It's going to be dark soon."

"Apollo?" Fontus questions.

"One more hour of walking, and then we'll find dinner."

We walk on in silence for another hour. I'm starting to get very worried that I'm slowing the men down. Maybe they'll be quicker if I wasn't with them. I should have gone back into the sea and sought help while they found the children.

"Ok, time to rest for the night." Apollo points toward a cave in the side of the mountain. "That looks like a suitable place."

"Good idea," Fontus agrees and helps me up to the cave. We enter the eerie darkness. I can hear dripping from somewhere deeper into the void. "We need some light."

"I'd really like my powers right now. That would help," Apollo laments.

"We'll just have to do everything the old fashioned way," I say, picking up two stones and handing them to Fontus. He looks down toward them as if they are poisonous.

"What am I supposed to do with those?" He passes them to Apollo who looks equally confused.

"My father is a rich lawyer, Eva. How the hell do we make fire out of stones?" Apollo inquires.

I roll my eyes. "You scrape them together to create sparks that will ignite the wood."

They both look at me as though I've gone insane.

"I'll fetch wood and then prepare some food for dinner," I tell them before leaving them alone together and dipping outside to collect logs and twigs. The birds tweet a good night high above me as they fly away to their evening of slumber. I begin to gather pieces of firewood. This island is beautiful, and in another time, I would have adored living here. The sun is low in the sky now, and for a few moments, I stand and watch it disappear over the horizon, the colors surrounding it vibrant and intoxicating. For the first time in days, I feel relaxed but still a little bundle of nerves sits in my stomach when I think about what will happen in the coming days. The sights we may find ahead could destroy us.

A loud roar startles me out of my reflection. I can't see where it's coming from, but I hope to god we don't encounter it. It doesn't sound like anything I've heard before: neither wild animal nor human. I hold the small bundle of firewood tightly in my arms and scamper back to the cave.

Apollo and Fontus are sitting on the ground with a piece of dried moss placed between them. They are both furiously trying to get the stones to spark. I laugh at them and deposit the wood on the floor. Going to the bag I packed earlier, I pull out some matches.

"You men are useless. We'll do it the easy way instead."

"You had matches all along?" Apollo frowns at me, a flash of annoyance transforming into a smirk.

"Always! My father taught me to prepare well."

"He should have taught my father that too," Apollo sighs. "Considering the strength of their friendship, our parents couldn't be more vastly different."

Neptune and Jupiter have been best friends since the earliest days of the gods. Many of the stories that the humans recount about them call them proper brothers, but they're not—they're just very close. I remember traveling to Rome to visit Jupiter and his family. Although Apollo's twin sister was there, he wasn't. He remained a mystery to me back then. The first time I actually met him was when he turned up on this island.

"How is your father coping with the increase in Pluto's activity recently? My father told me about Mars and Venus," I ask.

"He's got us all very busy. He's still recovering from the injuries inflicted on him by Mars," Apollo replies.

We manage to start the fire, and both men sit down. I open the bag, and removing the food, I lay it out in front of us. There isn't much as I'm trying to ration it: some bread, cheese, ham, fruit, and vegetables. I reach for the papaya.

"There were lots of reports about Mars injuring his father. It must've been hard for all those involved," Fontus joins in as he picks up some bread and cheese.

I remember the reports he's talking about. It wasn't that long ago. In order to save Venus, Mars had been forced to kill his father. Thankfully, Jupiter survived. There was talk of Mars being banished after the incident.

"Why wasn't Mars sent away?" I ask taking a bite of ham.

Apollo reaches out for his own helping of bread and ham before he responds. "My mother got involved. She says that all her sons will understand the worry of their father when they find the woman they love. It's why my brother is now married with a baby on the way. It's supposed to be more of a punishment for Mars than banishment would've been. I don't think I get it ... unless all the dirty diapers he'll soon be changing count as a form of torture."

"Yes, that sounds like Hell." Fontus laughs and lays back on the ground.

The cave has warmed up now the fire is raging. Its orange glow casts a light around the cavern, and I can see markings on the walls. I'm intrigued to look at them further. I leave the men eating, and getting to my feet, I pick up a stick with some moss at one end and dip it into the fire.

"Where are you going?" Apollo immediately stands to attention.

"Nowhere. I just want to take a closer look at the markings in the cave."

"Don't wander too far," Fontus warns and throws a grape in his mouth.

"I won't," I promise them and take my makeshift torch over to the walls. The drawings appear to be very old. They're etched into the walls with charcoal and also what I can sense is a water content. I follow one of the drawings along the wall.

"What are they of?" Apollo calls after me.

"It looks like there could be a waterfall deeper into the cave. I can see an illustration of an inlet. I did feel the presence of its dampness when I first entered, but I thought it was just a musty cave. There are sea creatures shown as swimming in there."

"Maybe if we can locate them, they can find a way to dive deep and call your father?" Fontus suggests.

I study the pictures in more detail, looking at the creatures. I recognize the majority, but one seems scary. A large dragon-like fish with teeth and spiny gills. From the depiction of the encounter, it appears that the creature could shoot the gills and puncture straight through a human. I had wanted to visit the waterfall but maybe staying away might be a better idea.

"Do they indicate whether the water leads to the other side of the island?" Apollo asks as he appears at my shoulder.

His hands rest around my waist, and I can't help thinking about what it would be like to feel him moving inside me in the same way Fontus does. Is the spell taking over again, or is it my natural curiosity? Apollo smiles down at me, and I feel a heat run through me. Shaking it off, I return to studying the drawings.

"Look, there's our cave." I point to where the opening is situated at the foot of the mountains. I follow the markings with my finger. "It looks like the mountains get harder to climb this way, but this other way, shown as longer, seems easier. A lake lines the route, so I can always bind the water to my will and control it. The only problem would be what looks like a volcano."

"I wouldn't say that's the only problem." Apollo points at a figure drawn on what I'm assuming is a map. "What is that?" he asks.

"I'm not sure—it's why I skipped over it. It looks like a man with a club, but when you look at his proportions in relation to the mountains, he'd be too big."

"An ogre big or giant big?" Fontus is still lying on the floor, resting with his eyes shut, and his strong arms behind his head.

"Is there are difference?" I ask. Both would scare me if I were to encounter them.

"Ogres are known for being more stupid, but equally they are more likely to eat you." Fontus' reply makes me anxious.

"Shut up. You'll scare her," Apollo scolds the other half of my men and wraps his arms tightly around me.

"Are we going that way?" I worry at my lip. Being dinner for an ogre isn't high on my list of priorities.

"I think it could be the best option. You aren't going to be able to go the mountain route unless we find a pair of left-over shoes somewhere. Besides, as you've already mentioned, it's close to water, so hopefully we can call upon your magic to protect us."

I look back at the map and smile at the thought of the protection I can give us all.

"How are you coping without your powers, Apollo?"

"It's strange. So many things I'm used to being able to do, and now I can't."

"Doesn't music provide the essence of your abilities?"

"Yes, there's nothing more special to me than listening to people expressing themselves through chords." Apollo runs his hand through his blond hair.

"We'll have to find some music to see if it can restore your powers." I press a kiss to his lips, and he holds me closer.

"It won't. I've already experienced music while being here. You, me, and Fontus together create a melody in my head, but my powers haven't returned." He looks forlorn.

"Coventina said you still have them—you just haven't realized it yet." I wish I understood the meaning of the old lady's words. At present, they confuse me.

"I hope my powers show themselves soon then." Apollo strokes down my face, and I feel the magic of the island drawing us together once again

"Shush." Fontus suddenly appears behind us. His eyes wide with panic. "There's something outside."

The roar I heard earlier, the alien sound of neither human nor beast, comes from just outside the cave.

"Apollo? What do we do?" Fontus pulls me behind him.

"Can you two call on the water?" Apollo looks frantically around.

"No. We're too far away." I raise my hand and will water to come to me but nothing happens.

Apollo inhales deeply as the last embers of my torch burn down to nothing.

"We must go farther into the cave then."

FONTUS

Chapter Twenty One

Using dirt from the ground, we hurriedly put out the fire. Whatever is outside could be attracted to the light if it hasn't already caught our scent. Another inhuman sound breaks the silence of the night beyond the mouth of our shelter. Louder this time. Closer.

A thin beam of light suddenly cuts through the darkness.

"I have a flashlight," Eva whispers. "Come on."

Apollo takes the lead, Eva in the middle while I follow behind them. Even though she has her powers, in this forma-tion we can protect her if needed. We don't know what we face ahead of us. I'm not sure being out in the wilderness of the island is better than the house. At least there we had food and a bed.

Memories of what Ambrose did to me rise to the surface, and I battle down a bout of nausea. Maybe facing a beast would be better than seeing the principal again. He was pure evil.

Fingers brushing over the rough rock wall, I follow the others with my ears straining for sounds behind us.

No one speaks.

We move as silently as possible.

Eva flicks the flashlight slowly from side to side when the

tunnel eventually widens. A soft luminous glow emanates from farther along, and the sound of rushing water increases as we move steadily closer.

Eva makes a small sound of excitement.

Smiling, I feel it too. It's part of us … it's who we are. That will never change. Just the thought of sinking into its coolness has my skin tingling.

Reaching a bend, Apollo moves ahead first.

"Wow!" I hear him exclaim.

Eva and I then turn the corner, and we both stop in our tracks.

Phosphorescent moss illuminates a cavernous grotto in blue. An underground waterfall cascades forcefully into a large clear lake below.

"It's beautiful!" Eva utters, switching off the flashlight and stowing it in her pillowcase bag.

"We still need to be careful," I point out. Although my expression's unable to hide my own delight.

Apollo intently sweeps the scene with his eyes. "Look, there's a path cut into the rock. We can follow it down to the bank."

"What about the creature from the cave painting?" Eva asks.

"Those paintings looked pretty old," I tell her, curving my arm around her waist and giving her a squeeze. "The water's clear, and there's no sign of anything. It probably died a long time ago."

Apollo hums in his throat. "Let's stay alert, just in case."

Using the wall for support, we scramble down the crude steps that have been chiseled into the rock face. Someone had gone to a lot of trouble to put them there. Such a perfect source of water must have been important to the natives of the island. I wonder where they are now? Slaughtered by Pluto and his minions? Or used for his insidious plans?

"Ouch." Eva gasps, suddenly jerking up her foot. "The rocks are sharp on my bare feet."

Crouching down, I check her sole and find blood seeping from a nasty cut. "I'll need to wrap it in some material when we get to the bottom of the steps to protect it until it's healed."

Apollo turns and scoops her up into his muscular arms.

"Fontus, take the lead. I'll carry her."

Eva pouts with annoyance but doesn't complain. Giving her an amused look, I move to the front. We both agreed to follow the blond god's leadership, but I know she doesn't like being treated like a helpless female.

On reaching the bottom of the steps, the ground is sandy. There's no sign of danger. Nothing stirs, and a strange sense of peace washes over me.

"All clear," I call as Apollo negotiates the final steps with the beautiful sea goddess still held tightly in his arms.

Gently lowering her to the sand, he lifts up her foot to inspect it. Crimson oozes from the clean slice in the flesh close to her big toe. I'm actually surprised she's lasted this long without injury, considering the terrain we've been traveling over.

"Ouch!" she complains and gives him a glare. He grabs the pillowcase she's been using to carry her things, and with a knife, he cuts a long strip from the top of it.

"The water will help heal her quicker," I tell him, and taking the material from him, I walk over to the lake. Kneeling at the edge, I immerse the cloth. Cool liquid washes over my fingers. It brings with it an echo of my powers from deep inside my soul. I want nothing more than to sink into the depths but know that's not possible until we've helped Eva.

An odd clicking noise from above has the blood turning icy in my veins. My head darts up in time to see a creature poised at the top of the carved steps. Pincers open and close around its gaping fanged mouth, and bulging black eyes are stationed on either side of its bulbous head. The rest of it is revealed as it squeezes itself down our only exit. A lion-like body is attached to the mismatched head. It has large paws and golden fur that end at its midsection. The bottom half is that of a bear.

"What the hell is that?" I question, racing back to Eva.

Apollo's expression is a picture of shock. "It looks like someone has made their own version of a chimera."

A guttural cry comes from the creature's throat, and with a speed that shouldn't be possible for something so large, it charges down the steps toward us.

Eva raises her hands. I sense her powers humming to the surface, but before she can call the water to protect us, the creature lands on Apollo tearing at him with its pincers and unsheathed claws.

APOLLO

Chapter Twenty Two

Pain screams though my chest. Grappling the beast's throat, I prevent it from savaging my face.

It's a monstrosity and surprisingly strong. A jumble of creatures that are not meant to be melded. Through magic or some other nefarious source, someone has perverted nature.

Fontus gives a cry and running over to Eva, he grabs her under the arms, and hauls her clear. I can see her hand outstretched ready to help me yet hesitant, fearing she might hurt me with her powers in the struggle.

Saliva drips from the monster's jaws, and my arms tremor with the effort of keeping it at bay. My strength is usually enough to toss such foes away, but this thing seems to have been built with the force to bring down gods.

"Apollo." Eva's shout is desperate.

"Do it," I holler, a burning sensation spreading from the wounds I've already suffered.

An explosion of water hits from the side. The blow is enough to dislodge the beast, sending it flying into the cavern wall. Drenched with cold water, I'm left gasping. Rolling up onto my feet, I ignore the blood running from the slashes on my chest. I need to stay focused. This thing needs to be destroyed before I worry about my injuries.

Fontus edges to the left of me, the knife in his hand, ready to fight. Hissing, the creature rights itself and swings around to confront us. It's pincered maw works faster … we've pissed it off. This time, it springs at my companion. Fontus is quicker, and leaping clear, he slices the chimera's side with the knife, leaving a jagged slash. It screams in a mix of pain and rage.

Instead of retreating as I expect, it turns its attention on Eva. In a blur of unnatural movement, it swipes a mighty paw, missing her by inches. With a fierce look, the little sea goddess lashes out with her powers. Water rises in a wave from the lake and slams into the monster.

Concentrating, I try to call on my own abilities, but once again, something I don't understand blocks them. I lack the celestial music that my inner energy is drawn from.

"It's not stopping," Fontus points out as the creature once more finds its feet. "It's like its wired to keep on going, no matter what."

"Maybe it is. The whole island is designed to keep us breeding and only in certain locations. Perhaps this is some sort of watch dog, placed here to stop prisoners crossing the boundary from one area to the next," I suggest.

Eva brushes some loose hair out of her eyes, watching it cautiously. "Why didn't you see it before, when you came looking?"

"I wasn't out here at night, and I didn't travel this far," I remind her.

Shaking its insect like-head from side to side, the creature bares its fangs aggressively. Whatever drives it is strong, and it's not stupid—I can see calculation gleaming in its black eyes.

A bout of dizziness has me swaying on my feet. Raising a

shaking hand, I gingerly touch my bloodied chest. I'm still losing blood. From the fire raging through my nerve endings, I know its pincers must be poisonous. Being a god, it shouldn't be fatal. Yet here on this island, nothing is for certain. Finding my resolve, I ignore the pain. Fontus and Eva come first. Even if I lose my own life, I will not allow them to lose theirs.

"Don't let it scratch you," I advise as it begins to stalk around us.

Eva tosses me a worried look but doesn't reply. I don't need them worrying over me now and putting their own lives at risk.

One second, it's prowling, and the next, it's airborne, bearing down on me. I hit the sandy ground hard as it slams into me, its weight stealing my breath. Shielding my face with my forearm, its fangs penetrate the flesh. There's no holding in the scream as agony radiates through my arm.

"No." Fontus appears beside me.

Thrusting the knife deep into its neck, he withdraws the blade only to stab it again, over and over. The power behind the jaws clamped to my limb doesn't lessen, though, if anything it tightens.

"Run," I shout my voice high and shrill. "Fontus get her the hell out of here. Get in the water."

Eva's sudden scream is mingled with a thunderous roar. Turning my head, I discover the source. Another creature has found us. Coiled up out of the water, the leviathan's body is long, shimmering with blue scales. Gills are spread from either side of its neck, quivering aggressively. It's snout-like mouth opens to reveal bone-white teeth that gleam in the blue glow, surrounding us.

"Fontus," I yell.

Abandoning his place beside me, knife still in his hand, Fontus dashes to grab Eva.

The Chimera shakes its head, my arm still locked in its jaws. I feel the tendons stretching to breaking point, and my shriek mirrors my torment. Ramming my fist into its left eye, I keep hitting it, hoping for some relief.

EVA

I can't do more than stare open mouthed as the leviathan appears out of the water, his razor sharp teeth trapping me in a frozen stance. During my time in the sea, I've seen many mystical creatures of the deep but never anything like this. I'm terrified. I can vaguely hear Apollo's shouts of pain coming from behind me. I'm powerless to help him, though, as the creature lowers its head toward me, and its long snakelike tongue darts out of its mouth and licks its scaled lips.

"Eva." Fontus slams into me, and wrapping a strong arm around my waist, he pulls me out of the way, just in time, as the creature dives at the exact spot I'd been standing. We tumble onto the ground and roll against the wall. Jagged edges of the rock face scrape at my skin. The leviathan announces its anger at not catching me for its dinner with a loud roar that echoes throughout the cave.

"We have to stop it." Fontus is breathless as he gingerly gets up to his feet and holds his stomach.

"How?" I stumble up to mine, my left ankle hurting where I hit it against the wall.

"Remember that game we used to play as kids." Fontus smirks and starts to roll his hands together.

"Which one?" I wrack my brains, trying to work out what he means, but I can't think of anything. When he summons a long strand of water out of the underground lake, I catch on to his meaning. "Capture Daddy!" I smirk, knowing exactly what he plans.

The creature lunges for us again, and we both scatter to either side of the water. I call forth the water, turning it into a rope. Commanding the twisted stream of liquid, Fontus and I both start to wind it around the sea creature. It doesn't realize what we are doing at first and continues to make lunges toward us, hoping to enjoy us for a snack. On land, we are quicker than it, though. Eventually, the rope's wrapped around its entire body, and the creature's eyes widen, wondering what's happening. It thrashes hard in the water, desperately trying to escape, but we have it bound tightly. It tries to make a dive for us again, its sharp teeth and strong jaw snapping wildly. When it realizes it can't get to us, it tries to dive into the water but can't escape us when we control the clear liquid surrounding it.

"You know, I once asked Neptune what would happen if we pulled the water too tight." Fontus shouts at me from the other side of the lake.

"Yes. He said it would tear him apart," I reply, my eyes never leaving the deadly mouth of the creature. I can still hear Apollo's painful cries to my left, but I can't do anything to help him at the moment. I need to keep my focus on the water creature. Whatever Pluto has done to this island, he's created a trap to keep us all breeding for his army. To come this way may have been a mistake, but I'm not going to give up. I'm not the weak woman everyone makes me out to be. Currently I'm the strongest in the room, and I have a man … no, two men to save.

"Do it," I shout adamantly at Fontus, tightening my fingers into a ball, willing the water to constrict the creature tighter and tighter. It begins to cut off its breathing. However, there's something else about the properties of water when it's formed into a rope. It's sharp, and the creature starts to cry out in agony as the bindings around it start to cut into its scaly flesh. Green blood flows from the wounds as Fontus and I will the water to squeeze tighter and tighter. The leviathan cries for mercy, but we know that if we show any we'll be eaten. On this island, it's one against one—no clemency can be given once an individual's true colors are shown.

In a last ditch attempt, the leviathan shoots sharp spikes from its gill as illustrated in the pictures on the cave walls above us. I'm thrown backward as one hits me, and I momentarily loose concentration on the water. I don't feel any pain, and taking a quick look over my body, I see the spike has gone through the knot in the sheet I wear across my shoulder. I'm left hanging on the wall with my feet dangling, but I'm not hurt. The sea creature cries out, and I quickly refocus on the water and start to squeeze it again. On the other side of the lake, Fontus is kneeling down on one leg. A spike sticks out of his other one, but otherwise he looks uninjured.

"Tighter," he shouts, and I curl the water over the Leviathan's gills so it can't do the same again.

My hands are squeezed so tightly now I can feel my nails digging into the flesh of my palm. "Come on, come on," I whisper to myself. The creature thrashes around in so much pain now. The ropes of water have met bone. It's dying but is still strong enough to kill us if we let it go.

"One last push," Fontus shouts, and I allow the water to

completely take over my body in a way I've never done before.

The spike holding me falls out of the wet wall behind me. I'm at one with the water now—a goddess controlling it without thought. I raise myself high in the cave, the water launching me on a platform akin to a crystal clear throne. My father spoke of the power and sovereignty in the sea, and for the first time ever, I realize what he means.

I'm in front of the sea creature now. It snarls and tries to spit at me, but I click my fingers, and the ropes surrounding it cut straight through, leaving the creature in little pieces on the floor. Green blood splatters on my dress and face, but I twist my hand around, and the liquid remnants of the creature wash away, leaving my sheet dress glowing white. My water platform lowers me down to Fontus, and he helps me step off it. With another click of my fingers, the remainder of the sea creature disappears into the water, leaving the cave clean.

"Ok, what the fuck just happened?" Fontus stares at me.

"I think I just embraced my inner water goddess."

We both turn sharply as Apollo screams, and the chimera attacking him roars victoriously.

"No." We both run toward our companion. The water races past me, heading for the creature. It doesn't reach it, though, for out of the shadows, a third monster appears. A giant at least twice our size, he wields a wooden club embedded with iron points like nails. He looks down at us with his one eye before swinging the club above his head, and bringing it down straight into the body of the chimera.

All I can do is scream.

FONTUS

I'm not entirely certain what I've just witnessed, coming from Eva. I've only ever seen control over water like that from one other person before, and that's her father: the King of the Sea. I'm not sure if I should be elated or terrified. She's finding new strength on this island, hidden in the depths of her soul. I just hope she'll be able to return to the Eva I know when she leaves, and the sorrows she's seen and felt don't destroy her. The leviathan is dead. I'm injured, again, but we now need to save Apollo. The chimera stands over his battered, bleeding body. My first thought is to flood the water over the creature to destroy it, but we don't get a chance when the gigantic figure appears. My sense of victory at beating one creature deflates until I watch the enormous cyclops send his club into the body of the chimera.

"Move," the cyclops orders us in a deep voice, which sounds menacing in the cave. He swings again at the chimera, and the creature's pincers flare. Its fanged mouth roars out a warning to the cyclops to stop—he doesn't, though. Instead, he sends his club back into the creature's face. The chimera pounces at the cyclops, and they begin to trade blows. The distraction has worked, and Apollo is forgotten. Eva calls the water forth and cocoons the broken god in it, protecting him while we join the cyclops in his fight. I form my own water club and send it into the back of the chimera's head. He turns, snarling at me and is rewarded for his momentary distraction with two quick blows to the head from the cyclops. His pincers break, and he howls in pain.

Eva sends another thundering blast of water into the chimera, and the creature hits the wall hard and falls to the ground. The cyclops steps closer and raises his club, but the golden lion paw strikes out at the giant's leg. Eva twists her hand, and water manacles bind all four of the chimera's legs and shackle them to the ground.

"Must die," the cyclops says. "Mine."

"Please, be our guest," Eva replies.

The cyclops delivers five quick smashes into the chimera with his club. The creature tries to rear up again. But it loses the fight when the sixth blow descends, and it takes its last breath. I fall to the ground with exhaustion and blood loss, but then quickly get up when the cyclops bears down on Eva with his club raised.

"Human?" the giant asks.

Eva shakes her head.

"I'm a demigoddess of the sea."

"Bad one?" The cyclops raises his club, and I prepare to send a blast of water into him if he goes to hurt her.

"No, a prisoner here like the others."

The cyclops looks at her and sniffs, his one eyes focused intently on her.

"Hurt by the bad man who take my home?"

Eva brings her hands down in front of her and wrings them together nervously. What Pluto did to her still weighs heavily on her mind despite the magic of the island drawing us together.

"Pluto hurt me badly."

The cyclops nods and lowers his club.

"Friend?" he asks.

"I would like that." Eva holds her hand out to the cyclops, and he shakes it. His massive fingers wrap around Eva's tiny ones, dwarfing them.

"Me called Nalos," the giant informs us. "Men, good or bad?"

I get to my feet and go closer to where Nalos still holds Eva's hand. It's a protective gesture now, and I worry for a moment he's fallen under the spell of the island and will try to take her from me.

"They are good." Eva turns to where Apollo is still cocooned in the water. She waves her free hand, and the watery protection lowers him to the ground and flows away, leaving Apollo unmoving and bloody on the floor. My heart skips a beat seeing him that way. He's our strength, but at the moment he looks weak, half dead.

"He sick?" Nalos questions, and both Eva and I run to Apollo's side. I check first for a pulse. It's weak but still there.

"He's really hurt." Eva surveys the slashes across his chest and arm with the skin torn aside and bleeding. "I don't know how to fix this."

"Can you clean out his wounds with your powers and make sure there's no dirt in them?" I ask, and she nods. "We need to get some warmth in here too." I look toward Nalos, hoping he'll be able to start a fire for us.

"No." He shakes his head and closes his eye.

"Please," I plead with him as Eva starts to wash out Apollo's wounds.

"He sick." Nalos repeats. What is he trying to say to me. Why can't I understand him?

"I don't understand. Please, explain more."

Nalos goes over to the now dead chimera. I follow him.

"Bad, bad, creature."

"You don't need to tell me." I can't help but say a little prayer in my head for Apollo. As a god, he should be immortal, but on this island he may not be. He chose to stay with us knowing that he was powerless. I hope he hasn't sacrificed himself, trying to find out what Pluto is doing with the children he's breeding.

"No, bad, bad, creature. These." Nalos taps at what remains of the creature's pincers with his club. "Bad."

"They're what has hurt Apollo. They caused the marks on his body."

The Cyclops nods his head in agreement.

"Make friend sick."

"Yes, they've injured him. We need to get him warm, and his wounds cleaned. Will you help me by lighting a fire?"

"Won't help." Nalos is still being obstinate, and it's really starting to grate on me. All I want to do is save the man I care for, but I can't without the giant's help. I can barely walk. My leg is hurting so much I'm unable to go out of the cave and get more kindling to start a fire.

"Please. I don't want him to die." The words leave my lips in a desperate plea before I can withhold them.

"Love him?" Cyclops looks at me in confusion.

"I love them both," I freely admit.

"Bad, bad creature." Nalos looks sadly down at the chimera. He bites his lip, and it seems to me as though he's thinking about something, but I can't make out what. He takes his club and hits one of the pincers—a black liquid oozes from it, and I reach out to touch it, intrigued by the jet colored flow.

"No, bad, bad, friend sick, bad, bad." Nalos places his club between me and the flow. He points at the contents of the pincer and then at Apollo. "Bad, sick, friend dead."

I desperately try to figure out what he's saying. The creature attacked Apollo. It created his wounds. I repeat the cyclops words back in my head.

'Bad, sick, friend dead.'

It's then that it dawns on me what he's trying to say.

"This is poison?"

He nods.

"Eva makes sure you clean the wounds out well. They are poisoned."

"No good," Nalos informs me. "Need good."

"Is there an antidote? Where is it?"

Nalos looks toward the lake.

"Down." He points to the lake and motions swimming. "Deep leaf."

"There is a plant in the lake that will save him?" I ask.

Nalos nods his agreement.

I push up to my feet and hobble over to the lake. The water is no longer crystal clear, and I can't see to the bottom. The blood of the dead leviathan has stained it a muddy green.

"Eva, keep cleaning Apollo's wounds. Nalos, please, start a fire to keep everyone warm."

This time the cyclops agrees.

"I'll be back as soon as I can?"

I prepare to dive into the water, hoping my injured leg will allow me to swim. All I can think of is saving Apollo. I have to trust that Nalos is telling me the truth and won't hurt

Eva when I'm gone. Mind you, with her current abilities, her powers are stronger than they've ever been, so I think she'll be safe.

"Wait." Eva touches my shoulder. "Let me go. I can swim faster."

"No, stay with Apollo. You can protect him better than me from anything else that may appear."

"And what if there are other leviathans in the water?"

I laugh.

"When has anybody or anything ever out-swum me?"

"Be careful." Eva stands on her tiptoes and presses a kiss to my lips.

"Look after him for us."

"I will..." her voice cracks as she speaks.

I can't bear to see her cry now, so I turn away and dive straight into lake. I don't know what is down there, but I have to find the cure to heal Apollo.

Diving deeper and deeper, I see bits of the dead leviathan floating past me. Little fish swim up to the flesh. A couple take a bite but quickly swim away. It's hopefully a good sign that there's nothing else carnivorous in the water. Eventually I reach the bottom of the lake. Just as Nalos said, there is a green plant growing there. I grab a handful of leaves and prepare to go back to the surface when a movement of a larger scale catches my eye. A nest of baby leviathans stare out at me. Their mouths open, squawking for food. My instant thought goes to the sea creature we killed. Was it the mother or the father? I push off the lake bed in a hurry and swim as fast as I can back to the surface. When I get to the top, a fire is already burning. Eva stands over Apollo, her eyes red-rimmed with tears. Nalos is nowhere to be seen.

I climb out of the lake and hand her the plant. She starts to lay it over his wounds, pushing it into the deep cuts.

"Where is our new friend?" I ask, standing by the fire to dry myself off. She points to the chimera now missing one of its bear hind legs.

"He pulled the leg off and mumbled something about 'more bad, protect friends'. I think he's standing watch at the mouth of the cave."

"I'm glad he's on our side."

"Me too." Eva finishes placing the leaves on Apollo's wounds before reaching over to check his pulse. Her face goes white, and she moves to another point. She places her hand over his mouth and turns to me, tears streaming down her face. My world falls apart in that instant for I already know what she's about to say.

"We're too late, Fontus. He's stopped breathing."

APOLLO
Chapter Twenty Five

A blue glow bathes me—my body feels light as a feather. Awareness seeping in, I find myself hovering in the air. Eva is weeping, tears trailing down her beautiful face, her body bowed in inner pain. Beside her, Fontus falls to his knees, his own eyes glistening as tears break free. He gives a cry of torment.

Panicked by their distress, I turn my attention to the body beneath me. No heartbeat sounds in its chest. No breath leaves its nose or lips. The pale handsome man has no flicker of life about him. There's something familiar … his features remind me of somebody, but my fog-filled mind doesn't recognize who.

"No." Eva grasps the dead man's shoulders. Leaning over him, she kisses his lips with her tear stained mouth. "You can't leave us. Please, not when we've just found you."

My lips tingle with sensation. It feels strange.

Fontus takes the corpse's hand, kissing it gently before laying it against his cheek. "Come back, please come back."

Flexing my hand, I feel the sense of someone's fingers around mine.

Confusion thickens inside my skull. Memories fade. What had I been doing? Who are these people, and why am I here? I don't understand. I needed to do something. It was important.

Snagging on to that certainty, I tightly keep a hold of it. I need help.

Before I even realize it, I'm flying fast and high. The world passes around me in a blur of color, sound, and movement. Just as quickly, everything stops. Hovering again, I glance around the room. I'm in a rustic villa. Beyond the window, I can see a sprawling vineyard—the thick green vines are heavy with grapes.

"You're going to be the death of me, beauty."

The sound of the lust-filled male voice catches my attention. Gliding from the room, I float through the open door, across the hallway, and into a bedroom. A couple are in the middle of fucking on the bed. The man is thrusting hard and fast into the heavily pregnant woman, his backside clenching with each movement.

The blonde beneath him moans. Her long legs are wrapped around his waist, and her dainty hands claw at his back. "Harder, Mars! Fuck me harder!"

"We're going to break the bed again," he warns, drilling her deeper. "And I don't want to hurt the baby...."

"It's fine, trust me," she growls, her fingernails drawing blood along his shoulder blades. "If you stop now, I will kill you!"

Shuddering, he quickens his pace, sending the bedframe rattling. Just as predicted, there's the sound of cracking as the legs on one side of the bed give out. As the mattress falls downward into a wonky slant, they both start laughing.

I know this man.

Mars.

My brother.

I'm the god Apollo, and if I'm not mistaken, I've just died. Fuck.

Eva and Fontus!

The thought of them alone on the island in danger tears me apart. I need to find them help. Did our message reach Neptune? My father? Did Pluto intercept it before it could reach them?

"Mars stop fucking your wife. I need your help!" I shout, but he doesn't seem to hear me. I roll my eyes. Of course, he can't talk to the dead. What I need is someone familiar with talking to spirits.

Gathering my ethereal energy, I center it on where I need to be. Time and space quicken around me in a dazzle of colors. When it finally lulls to a standstill, I'm in a room surrounded by masks with colorful beads adorning the walls. Selene's apartment in New Orleans is just the same as I left it.

The oracle herself is seated at a round table, a deck of tarot cards in her experienced hands, and her lips pursed. The tendrils of her deep red hair are tumbling into her eyes, escaping the headband she's slid on to contain it. Her flowing, blue cotton summer dress clings to her slender body, revealing every enticing curve.

"Well?" the woman opposite Selene asks, her tone laced in impatience. She is sitting in a chair that is tipped back, so she can rest her legs on the table with her ankles crossed. A top of the range crossbow rests on her lap, and she is dressed in combat pants and a green tank top. With her blonde hair tied up in a bun, and her blue eyes sparkling dangerously my twin sister, Diana, looks extremely annoyed.

Selene wets her lips nervously with the tip of her tongue. "The cards cannot find what you seek."

"Uh huh." The Goddess of the Hunt caresses her weapon. "Look, you're the closest thing I have to a celestial blood hound. I felt my brother's pain through our twin bond, which pisses me off to no end. I need to know where the idiot is, so I can rescue his irritating ass."

I make a scoffing sound. She's the infuriating one, not me, with her obsession for hunting and taking in stray animals including the shifting kind.

Selene's brows dip together. "I sense a spirit."

"Are you about to get possessed or something?" Diana questions, one fine eyebrow raising. "Just letting you know my trigger finger can get twitchy."

"No." The oracle shakes her head. "I sense … Apollo."

"Here? Now?"

"Yes."

My sister swears under her breath eyeing the room. "Why the hell am I not surprised?"

"Selene, can you hear me?" I ask, ignoring my twin and wishing it had been anyone else but her here in New Orleans.

Placing her fingers to her forehead, the red head closes her eyes. "I think he's trying to communicate with us."

"Well, what is he saying?" Diana snaps, dragging her feet off the table to land on the floor with a thud.

Selene's lips turn down in a grimace. "I don't know."

"I thought you were psychic!"

Eyes snapping open, Selene fixes them on the other woman with a glare. "I'm an oracle, and there's a huge difference in what I can tap into. I can't just wiggle my fingers and give you what you want."

"Then what use are you to Apollo now?"

The oracles eye's flash with a simmering anger. "You're a goddess, what about your powers, hmm?"

Sighing, my shoulders slump. Of course, my sister has to rub everyone she meets up the wrong way. Our looks are about all we share in the sibling department.

EVA

I don't know how long I lay cradled in Fontus' arms, drifting halfway between awake and crying for the loss of the man lying dead in front of us, but the sun now rises at the mouth of the cave. I thought it was the magic of the island that had given me the feelings of love I've developed for him, but it wasn't. It was my heart, and now it's broken. We should have left while we had the chance, saved ourselves, and allowed Jupiter and Neptune to come back to the island and destroy Pluto's plans, but we wanted to be heroes, and now we've lost the man who completes us.

Fontus strokes absentmindedly at the top of my head. I don't think he's slept much at all. He just sits staring at Apollo's body. His eyes are red rimmed from where he's been crying, immersed in his own feelings of loss.

"We should get moving. Nalos seems to think there are other chimera around here. Pluto must have created them to stop his prisoners wandering. They'll have discovered that we're missing by now and will be looking for us," Fontus speaks, but I sense no urgency from him to actually get going. If we could stay hidden away here in this cave forever, I think both of us would.

"I don't want to leave him." I press another kiss to Apollo's lips. They're cold now, his skin pallid. "Please." The sob is ripped from my mouth, and I can't stop the tears falling again. "What have we done Fontus? He came here to save us, and we ended up killing him. We should have left the island when we had a chance. He had no powers, but he stayed by our side. I don't understand it all. Why? Why has this happened? Why is Pluto doing all these terrible things?"

Tears are streaming down my face now. This is not a pretty cry—it's an ugly one. I'm broken, and I don't know how to carry on or to survive any longer. It's only been a few days, but in that time I've been raped, beaten, watched Fontus nearly die, and now I've lost Apollo. Am I such a bad person that I deserve all of this? I just want to rewind time and be back on the beach, collecting shells before I was taken. I don't think I can go on any longer. "Maybe we should just return to the house and do what Pluto wants of us? Coventina said Apollo had his powers. He just didn't know it. If he had them, though, he'd still be alive. Nobody on this island tells the truth. We were doomed the moment we set foot on it."

Fontus opens his mouth to argue with me, but no words come out. He's as broken as I am. His leg is now wounded, one of many injuries he's suffered on the island, and his rough treatment at the hands of Ambrose still weighs heavily on him.

"Let's stay here a little longer." He pulls me closer. We both lay there watching Apollo's body, willing it to move and hoping for a miracle to happen.

Eventually, I crawl forward and lay next to him. Fontus does the same on the other side. We wrap our arms around his cold body, and I allow my tears to fall onto his ivory skin.

"Please, don't let it be," I whisper against his chest. "Please, don't leave us."

My watery tears trickle down his chest, still covered in the green plant, the wounds no longer bleeding. One is directly above his heart. With my newly enhanced powers of control over water, I move my tears to form a heart shape over his no longer beating one. Fontus watches as his own tears fall.

"Our god of music, the sun, and healing. The world will be a duller place without you," I cry.

A blast of light shines in through a gap in the ceiling of the cave. It lands straight on the heart and illuminates the water, making it glow. All of a sudden, I'm blasted by the light. It infiltrates my body, flooding all my pores with a surge of power I've never felt before.

"Fontus," I call warily as I'm lifted off the ground. "What is this?"

He makes a grab for me, but the second he touches me, he starts to glow as well.

"Eva!" he shouts.

I can see him, but I can't stop what's happening to me. I'm rising higher and higher. Eventually, Fontus has to let go of me. When he drops back to the ground, my eyes go wide. All his wounds have healed. He looks completely healthy like he used to before he arrived on the island.

"I healed you," I spit out in disbelief.

He looks down at his body and to where the spiked gill of the leviathan was shot into his leg. There isn't even a scar showing now.

"What's causing this?" I'm scared. I can't control what's happening to my body.

"I don't know." Fontus shakes his head. He looks just as

worried as I am. He tries to reach for me again but is pushed back. Music suddenly fills the cave. Sensual and seductive, it fills me with a strange happiness. "Pluto must be doing something. Maybe he sensed your water powers. Fight it, Eva."

I'm high in the air now, and I feel content. I'm sure this isn't dark magic. It's coming from the light.

"It feels too good to fight," I tell Fontus.

"Eva, please. It'll be Pluto." He's racing up the steps to the upper levels of the cave to be nearer to me. "Fight it."

"Nothing that feels this good can be bad. Don't you see … music, healing?" I look up at the sun, and it bathes the entire cave in a warm light. "It's Apollo, his powers."

"Eva!" Fontus shouts at me, but I can't go to him. The thought of Apollo sends me flying forward through space.

I want to find him. The words are spoken in my head. I know this feeling. I'm teleporting. My father has helped me do it several times. I'm leaving the island behind. Apollo must still be alive somewhere if I'm leaving it. I just have to find him. "I'll be ok, stay safe. I'll return," I shout back toward Fontus, not knowing whether he'll hear me or not. All I know is there is warmth flooding my heart, and I have to go to its source.

When everything clears, I'm standing in a room full of masks and colorful beads on the walls. Two women stand in front of me with their mouths wide open. One with vibrant red hair is wearing a blue summer dress, and the other with blonde hair is dressed more casually in combat pants and a green t-shirt. I feel familiarity with the second, despite the fact she's glaring at me like she wants me dead for interrupting whatever conversation the two are having. I look around the room. Apollo's here. I can feel him, but I can't see him.

"Apollo?" I question nobody in particular. Maybe he's been projected into the body of one of these women? Possibly the second one who's now baring down on me with lips pursed. She wraps her hands around my neck and pushes me back against the wall.

"Where is my brother?" the woman asks, and it's then I recognize and remember her from previous meetings. She's Diana, Apollo's twin. Whatever power I have inside me has brought me to the closest living soul matched to Apollo's, and not the man himself. My entire body deflates, and my heart breaks for a second time that day.

"He's gone." I allow a single tear to drop down my cheek.

Diana releases me and steps backward.

"No, I would know. I felt pain, but I still feel him. He's alive." I shake my head.

"I've just left him in a cave on Pluto's island. He wasn't breathing."

"Where? Show me." She's desperate to get to him, but I can't risk taking her to the island. My powers are completely unbound there now, but hers aren't. She'll be powerless.

"I can't. It's too risky. We need to go to Jupiter and tell him." I start for the door, but she stops me.

"Who are you?" Diana asks.

"Eva, a demigoddess and the daughter of Neptune. We have met before."

"A demigoddess, yet you can teleport?" Suspicion laces the tone of Diana's words.

"I seem to have acquired Apollo's powers." I don't understand how I have these abilities, but if they will allow me to put a stop to what is happening on the island and save Fontus and by some miracle Apollo, then I'll do whatever it takes. "Please, I don't understand what's happening, but I love your brother. I've lost him, and I'm broken. He wanted the people of the island saved, and I want to do it for him."

"He's gone." Diana places her hand over her heart. Her own emotions erupting in a painful cry of loss. I want to comfort her, but I can't. I'll break again if I allow my path to be swayed from stopping Pluto.

The other lady, Selene, has been standing silently in the corner of the room during the entire conversation.

"The spirits told me this would happen. The island's so cold … magical. A creature created out of three different types attacked. Apollo thought himself invincible, foolish man. He died saving you and another." She stumbles over to a chair, the weight of what she's seen, leaving her weak.

"Fontus." I give Selene my other lover's name.

"A triangle of lovers. But Apollo feared to touch you because of the evil things you've had forced on you." I don't know who or what Selene is, but she knows so much.

"Lovers?" Diana interrupts.

"Please," I beg. I need to go to Jupiter.

Selene's eyes roll back in her head. She's seeing something else.

"What's happening?" Diana asks.

"Eva, I love you. I'm here." Selene's words have me taking a step backward. "Use my powers to rescue the children and Fontus. Live and love with him for the three of us."

"Apollo?" I question.

"I'm here in this room. I've not passed over. There may be a chance for me, but I don't know how, yet. Your strength allowed me to possess Selene. Diana, go to Jupiter. He'll know what to do."

"Apollo." I can barely speak. I'm so confused, elated, devastated—I don't really know what to feel at the moment, "Please, come back to me ... to us. We need you."

"I don't know my path, or where this spirit world's taking me. I'll be with you and Fontus always. Finish what we started. You have the strength. It's always been inside you."

"I can't do it without you. Please, Apollo. How can we save you?"

"There is a way. I need to seek the truth of it though. The island brought us together before it destroyed us—it can rebuild everything we have. It's magical for a reason. The source of its life is the key."

"I don't understand. What do you mean?"

"I don't know myself. Coventina was right. I always had my powers. I just didn't know it."

"Apollo, you aren't making sense. Explain more?"

Silence.

Nothing.

"Apollo?" I reach out and touch Selene's hand. "Please."

Her eyes return to normal, and she gasps for air.

"That was extraordinary. I've never felt anything like it before."

"Apollo?" I question again, hoping he'll come back.

"He's gone," Selene informs me.

"Gone?" Diana pushes me aside desperate to find out where her brother is. "Gone where?"

Selene shuts her eyes.

"Back to the island. He wants you to return there as well."

FONTUS

Returning from the lake, I drip fresh water onto the vibrant green leaves still covering the lacerations on Apollo's naked chest. The wounds still gape open, his lifeless form unmoving. Sitting beside him, I hold his hand and wait patiently for Eva's return. I trust her, but I hope she's safe. Whatever was happening, she was confident it would help us in some way.

Eva suddenly materializes out of nowhere. Her bedsheet clothing's now replaced with a pretty green cotton summer dress and a pair of flat leather sandals.

"What happened? Where have you been?" I demand, relief coursing through me at the sight of her.

"I found Apollo's sister, Diana. She's going to tell Jupiter and my father where we are. An oracle named Selene gave me a change of clothes before I returned."

"Does this mean you can teleport now? What about Apollo?"

Her expression drops into one of sadness. "Having teleported me, I felt his power ebb as I reformed. He ... he spoke to me. He's in the spirit world and doesn't know if he can ever return to us. He said to finish what we started and save the children."

Before my heart can break for a second time, the power

that had previously engulfed Eva swells up again. Gasping, the light hits both of us with the force of a tidal wave. The energy is immense. Divine. It encircles my being in warmth and a tranquility I've only ever experienced when basking in the sun. Entwining around us, it pulls us closer to Apollo's body.

Eva's small searching hand finds my bare chest.

We meet halfway, lips touching. Cupping her cheek in one hand, I taste her sorrow in our kiss. It isn't the magic of the island causing this. I feel it in my bones, and in my soul.

Whatever has us in its grip is purer … stronger.

Eva's tongue dances into my mouth, and the kiss deepens. Mindlessly, we cling to each other, still snuggling against our missing piece. The man I love. Whom I know Eva loves too even though she hasn't voiced it. I've seen the way she looks at him … the way she looks at both of us. What's between the three of us is more powerful than words. I fear without Apollo it might tear us apart forever.

"Fontus," she moans softly against my lips.

The power around us hums. It's not lustful like the enchantment back at the house, but it's just as potent in its sweetness. A combination of air, earth, water, and fire—this cavern amplifies the elements.

Fisting her hair, I swallow her breath on a rough kiss. The sunlight blazes brighter, becoming liquid heat around us, yet it doesn't burn. It cleanses our bodies. My hand moves to Eva's breast, and I fondle it through the material, finding the peak already hard and straining. There's no thought of worrying about Nalos walking in and catching us.

Eva's fingers tangle in my hair, and breaking the kiss, she brings my head down to her breast. I don't even hesitate. Pushing the cotton aside, I suck her nipple into my mouth.

She mewls and clenches my hair in her grip. Urgency drives me. Shoving my hand between her thighs, I find her pussy and tease it into excitement. Once she's wet enough, I thrust a finger inside her. Eva gyrates, fucking my finger as she reaches for the top of my shorts. Shoving them down over my ass with my free hand, I give her access to my steel hard cock.

This is madness.

We're mourning and shouldn't be doing this, but we just can't stop ourselves. I know the desperation written over her face mirrors my own. We're practically writhing on top of Apollo's corpse.

Curling her fingers around me, she pumps my length with her palm, smearing the pre-cum over the tip. Our moans and groans mingle with the sound of the waterfall still thundering into the lake while its waters lap gently at the bank. The music of nature. Of love.

The energy builds in its potency, higher and higher.

Taking Eva's other nipple into my mouth, I graze it with my teeth, making her cry out.

A sharp intake of breath startles both of us.

My attention jerking down, I see Apollo's chest rising and falling with no sign of the slash marks evident on his flesh. His skin is flushed, no longer pale and lifeless.

"He's alive! Apollo?"

He doesn't respond to Eva's hopeful call as her hand slips from my cock to touch his shoulder attentively.

Raising my head, I kiss his mouth lingeringly. "Apollo, I don't know how this is possible, but please, wake up."

Again, there's no response.

"I don't understand," Eva says, sounding panicked. "How did he come back? Why won't he open his eyes?"

We're both silent for a moment, trying to find the answer. Then it hits me.

"We're a triad. We're a perfect three," I point out in growing excitement. "I've heard legends about this but thought they were just stories."

"What are you talking about?" Eva asks with a look of confusion.

"We brought him back with our love and through the magic of us beginning to have sex." Cradling her breast again, I tweak her pebbled nipple. "We need to finish what we started and include him, or it will fade."

Biting her lip, her gaze falls to Apollo's tattered shorts. Without a word, she helps me unbutton them, and then we ease them down his hips, over his ass, and remove them. If we were worried about getting him hard, that's not a problem. The god's impressive cock is thickening and growing harder as we watch.

Gently taking a hold of it, I lick the end, flattening my tongue. Cupping his balls, Eva nuzzles them with her nose and uses her mouth to kiss the base of his cock. Licking, sucking, we worship his shaft until it's pulsing with a need for release.

Eva wastes no time straddling his hips, opening herself up to receive him. Keeping his cock in place, I grasp it while she slowly eases down onto him.

"Oh my." Eyes fluttering shut, her moan is breathy as she pushes downward, taking all of him until she's sitting on his groin. "Fontus?"

Petting her hair, I press a brief kiss to her mouth. "Bring him home to us."

Eva begins to move, riding him slowly, her breasts bouncing with the movements.

For a few moments, I watch, enjoying the show, before moving behind her and focusing on her ass. Positioning Eva forward, I suck my finger, and as I work it gently into her dark passage, she gives a sharp cry, but she doesn't tense up. We've experimented a few times like this in the past, and I know she can take me. Easing my finger in and out, a second joins it as I move them in a scissoring motion.

"Ready?" I ask.

Eva nods, still fucking Apollo's unconscious form. "I want you both. Please, Fontus, don't tease me."

Satisfied she's prepared enough, I press the crown of my cock into her and push in carefully. We both groan as I inch in slowly. I can feel Apollo's dick through the thin membrane separating us. Grasping her hips to steady myself, I thrust forward before finding our rhythm.

APOLLO

Chapter Twenty Eight

Neck arching on a crest of pleasure, my eyes snap open. The first thing I see is Eva above me, her brown hair rippling over her creamy shoulders, and her bare breasts bouncing as she rides my cock. Behind her, Fontus grunts as he pumps into her ass.

One second I'd been a drifting incorporeal spirit, lamenting over the immortal life I'd left behind, and the next it had all come screaming back into existence. It feels as if an invisible cord has yanked me backward with the force of a truck. Everything is heightened. Hearing, touch, smell, sight, taste. The senses that had been severed while I was dead are now amplified.

Reaching up, I take the heavy globes of Eva's breasts in my hands, rubbing the nipples with my thumbs. Lust laden eyes jerk to mine, a look of joy lighting up her expression.

"Apollo!"

"I'm going to come," I warn her, teeth gritted as I feel the tell-tale sign of lightening darting up my spine. But instead of getting off me like I expect, she grinds her hips down onto me harder. It's all too much. Balls tightening, my orgasm is raw and primal. Eva cries out as her pussy walls contract around my shaft, and she tips over the edge just as violently. Fontus groans at the same time, his body tensing, finding its own wild release.

Dazed, panting, I catch my little demigoddess in my arms as she crumples exhausted onto my chest.

"How the fuck did you just bring me back?"

Eva's smile is impish. "Sex magic."

My eyebrows shoot up into my hairline. "How did you even know about that?"

Fontus shrugs behind her, his body still shaking with the force of his orgasm. "Something in this place connected our powers … or maybe it's the emotions between us. Our grief at losing you. It triggered something among us and showed us how to revive you."

I don't know what to say to that. This connection between us goes way beyond all of us. If the magic enchantment holding this island hostage had something to do with sparking it, I am not ungrateful for it. A lump of emotion forms in my throat, but I swallow it down. They shared their energies to resurrect me. Do they realize how something like that would make us even more bound together? An inescapable binding that once sealed fully can never be broken. Do they not understand how dangerous it can be? Three immortals who would eventually need each other like air to breathe, and who would all be doomed if one of the entwined spirits was to die?

"My sister will have gotten word to my father and Eva's. We need to find those children before they descend on this place and start a war," I tell them, thoughts still heavy with worry for my two new lovers. Watching their grief destroyed me. I can't let that happen again. I refuse to be the cause.

We untangle ourselves, stripping off, and washing away

the scent of sex and pleasure from our naked bodies in the waters of the lake. They quickly fill me in on the appearance of Nalos, the cyclops, the death of the leviathan, and the poison in the chimera's pincers.

"Nalos might know where the children are being held," I suggest, pulling up my shorts and refastening them. "It's too dangerous, staying here any longer. Ambrose will know by now your missing, and when the chimera doesn't return to him, it will mean even more danger for us."

Eva slides the straps of her cotton dress up her bare shoulders, covering her breasts. "He's been outside guarding. We can ask him now."

Gathering our makeshift bags, we hurry up the carved stone steps, leaving the cavern and the secret waterfall behind us.

With Eva's fresh set of clothes and sandaled feet, we move a lot quicker than when we first entered. I catch her looking at me a few times and biting her lip. Maybe she expected something more heart felt when I awoke. Some stronger reaction. A repeat of the words of love I'd spoken to her while I was a spirit. No matter how much I love them both, I have to safeguard this mission and protect them. Even if that means breaking us apart.

"Fontus, once we've spoken to Nalos, I want you and Eva to go to the beach and return to the sea," I tell him with as much command in my voice as I can muster even though it hurts. "You're to return to Neptune's Kingdom and stay there until this is all over."

He blinks at me slowly, his expression mirroring Eva's surprise. "We need to finish the mission ..."

"No. I need to finish the mission. You both have to leave."

A small hand finds my arm, fingers digging into my skin. "You can't do that. Not after what we just went through."

Shaking off Eva's grasp, I stare down at her with every ounce of arrogance I possess. "I'm in charge. You'll both do as I say. Go home. I don't need either of you here. You're nothing but a distraction and a burden."

EVA

Fresh tears sting my eyes, and I turn away so Apollo won't see the pain he's causing me. Fontus purses his lips together, and red tints his face. He's angry and rightfully so.

"All right, we'll go." Fontus grabs my hand and starts to drag me along behind him. I dig my feet into the ground and refuse to move. Calling forth the water, I send it slamming into Apollo's chest. It drenches him and knocks him flat on his ass.

"You're an absolute bastard." I rip my hand from Fontus' and stomp over toward the shocked god sitting on the floor, wondering what just happened. I've figured Apollo's plan out, but it won't work. "Arrogant sod. I should push the water into your body and give you an enema … just because I can. I've got more power in my little finger than you have in your entire body at the moment. Your power surges through my body as well as the power of a water god. You think by pushing us away you are saving us from Pluto, but you are a complete idiot. Don't you get it? Without us as a triad, you'd be dead. We're in this together. It's not the magic of the island keeping us alive, it's the three of us together. You send us away, and you'll fail." I fold my arms across my chest and stare at him, my face a picture of fury.

I hear Fontus laugh behind me.

"She would give you an enema as well. She got into trouble as a kid for doing it to someone who was bullying her friend." Fontus wraps his arms around me. "I love you, my little spitfire."

Apollo shakes his head and looks guiltily at the ground.

"I'm sorry. I'm not used to caring this much for anyone. I'm a fuck them and leave them sort of guy. The image of something happening to you both popped into my head, and I dread it."

"Idiot," I mutter and resume my pouting.

"I agree. I am." Apollo gets up from the floor and comes closer to us.

He tries to take my arms and unfold them from my chest. I resist. I'm still angry at him. He looks at me with his big blue eyes, and I feel my anger melting away.

"I'm sorry. I give you my word we'll do this together. All three of us side by side. Let's finish what Pluto started. We've got people to save before war descends," Apollo confirms.

I wait a few seconds before bringing a smaller amount of water up and dropping it on his head.

"Last warning. Do something like that again, and it goes up your ass."

Apollo smirks.

"Promises, promises. When this is over, Eva, I'm going in your ass, darling."

I can't help but blush, all anger forgotten. I can still feel Fontus in there from earlier.

"We need to go before we end up fucking again. Jupiter will be on his way. He won't allow this island to remain standing for much longer." Fontus senses the rising sexual desire as his own cock lengthens against my back.

"Have you got control of your teleportation powers?" Apollo asks me as he leads us up the steps of the cave and out into the warm sunshine of the day.

"Sort of," I reply. "I'm not sure how to relocate to somewhere when I don't know what it looks like."

Nalos is sitting on a rock, cleaning his club. He looks up at us and grins when he sees all three of us.

"Friend not dead."

"Nope." Fontus smiles happily.

"Good."

"Nalos?" Apollo questions. "Do you know where the house is that holds the children?"

"Bad place."

"You've been there?" Apollo asks.

The cyclops nods his head.

"Can you remember it?"

"Yes. Can't forget." Nalos looks sad, and I go to his side and place a hand on his arm to comfort him. "Babies, mine, gone."

I tilt my head looking at him. We'd never asked why he was on the island and yet not under Pluto's power.

"This is your island. You were here before Pluto came?"

"Yes."

"You have a family?" I lower myself down onto the ground and sit at Nalos' feet. He looks directly at me. His one eye filled with the wetness of tears.

"Yes. Wife, baby," Nalos informs me. I swallow deeply, knowing what will come next. "Pluto take baby, kill wife."

I take his hand in mine.

"I'm so sorry."

"Want bad man gone."

"We all do." Apollo joins us. "We need to get to the house

where the children are without any further delays. Eva has the ability to teleport but will find it hard to go somewhere or to someone she's never seen. Will you allow her to look into your head for the house, so we can travel there?

Nalos nods his acceptance.

"Eva, place your hands on either side of Nalos' head. Relax and allow his thoughts to flow into your mind. See what he feels."

I do as Apollo instructs. At first, nothing happens, so I concentrate harder, and that's when the tears start to fall from my eyes. I see a family, a mother, father, and a son running around the island, enjoying life. The world grows dark, and a bolt of fire shoots out of the sky and kills the mother. The father is injured but doesn't die. He watches on as the boy is taken by Ambrose. I can barely breathe. This is not a power I want. Apollo can have it back. I want to control water—it doesn't hurt like this does. The vision changes, and I see the house. The father attacks but is beaten back. His son is screaming at him to save him. I can't watch anymore of this. I pull my hands away and burst into heart-breaking sobs. Fontus and Apollo both crowd around me, rubbing my shoulders and covering me with their warmth and comfort.

"It's ok," Fontus whispers into my ear before standing up and punching Apollo in the face.

"What the fuck did you ask her to do that for? You knew what she'd see."

Apollo rubs his jaw.

"It's the only way. This is why I wanted you to go back to the shoreline."

"I'm ok." I push away from them both and take strong

breaths to get some air into my lungs. Eventually, I manage to calm down. "I'm fine."

Turning to Nalos, I see the sad expression on his face.

"I'm so sorry you went through that. We'll get him back for you."

"If still alive," Nalos replies.

"I'm sure he is." I reach out and take his hand. "Ok, hold onto me everyone. I've seen the house so I can get us closer now."

"Keep the house in your head but imagine a place to either side of it. Preferably covered, so we can get our bearings and plan an attack without being seen. Our priority is going to be to find the children and get them out of there. Jupiter and the rest of my family are on the way. They'll deal with Pluto and the guards."

Apollo takes my hand and squeezes it tightly, giving me reassurance. Fontus takes my other, and Nalos places his hand on my shoulder. I shut my eyes and bring up an image of the house. I remember a patch of trees to the left of it. I focus on them, but as we start to teleport, I can't stop the vision of Nalos' son from entering my head.

FONTUS

The roar of a crowd goes up as we come out of the spin of the teleportation, and then it instantly goes quiet. Deathly silent. I dare to open an eye and peek out at the surroundings Eva has brought us to. We are in the middle of a large arena, the size of the Coliseum when it wasn't a ruin. We are surrounded by people of all shapes and sizes sat in the seats, staring at us with open mouths. On the ground beside us are several gladiators also confused by our sudden appearance. One boy, little more than twelve years old, stares at us with his one eye.

"Fuck," Eva exclaims.

"What did you think of?" Apollo steps in front of the woman we both love.

"Son," Nalos cries.

"What he said." Eva bites her lip nervously.

"Yeah not a particularly helpful thought at this time," I respond as I join Apollo in front of Eva. Both of us are playing protectors despite her wielding the greater powers. "What do we do now?"

"Get out of here. Take my hands again," Eva suggests.

"I think the element of surprise has gone," Apollo reluctantly admits. "I think we're going to have to fight."

A murmur goes around the crowd. From a vantage point in a box high up in the stadium, Ambrose watches on. He's standing next to Pluto, the God of the Underworld.

"Oh shit, Eva, go," I tell her.

"I'm not leaving you behind." She stands defiantly against the smirking face of the man who raped her.

"Well this is interesting." Pluto places a hand on Ambrose's shoulder, and the look on his face is nothing short of demonic. "I thought you said these two had disappeared? It seems they couldn't stay away, and I do believe they've brought me a fully-fledged god to play with as well. Apollo, good to see you again. You'll be a welcome asset to my breeding program. As you can see we're testing out some of the children today before they are sent on to the next stage of their training. Some are faring better than others."

My stomach lurches when I see several children on the floor. They're bleeding out from where they've been injured. Pluto clicks his fingers, and the young gladiators line up instantly. They've been trained to accept his every command, including Nalos' son. He's the last to join the line, staring a moment longer at his father as though he recognizes him from somewhere but can't place him.

"Nalos." I reach out when I hear the cyclops growl. "Wait. Please. You attack now, and Pluto has the power to strike your son down just like your wife. We'll make sure we walk away from this with him."

"Need, kill." Nalos snarls, his club held tightly in his hand.

"You'll get the chance," Eva reassures him with a calming touch to his shoulder.

"Get behind us, Eva," Apollo orders her back to where we can protect her.

She just raises an eyebrow at him. She's the one with the

power and won't let us treat her like the little woman any longer. She pushes her way in between the two of us, taking her place alongside us in a line.

"Whatever comes at us, we fight it together."

"Well, you're not the insipid little girl I fucked over my desk. I like this new version. I think I'll enjoy fucking you again once your companions are dead. We need to do something about the magic emanating from you first though."

Pluto points at Eva, and a magical blast comes out of his hand. It surrounds her in an energy ball. She shuts her eyes, and it disintegrates to nothing.

"What the fuck?" Pluto spits out in disbelief.

"Apollo gave me these powers and only he can take them away."

Eva takes the opportunity to send energy ball after energy ball toward Pluto and the rest of the occupants in his royal box.

"Release Cerberus," Pluto roars, and the gladiators scatter to the sides of the arena.

"Eva, stop," Apollo orders.

I've encountered Cerberus before. It's the hell hound, a three-headed dog that guards the gates of the Underworld. It's not something to be messed with.

Apollo flips an approaching guard over his shoulder and knocks him unconscious before grabbing his sword. "Nalos, go and fetch your son. We need to get out of here and wait for Jupiter to come."

"I'll help him," I tell Apollo who nods his agreement.

Following behind Nalos, I use the limited water supply in the stadium and form arrows to spear into the guards who charge for us. The cyclops swipes at them with his club.

"Release him, now," I hear Pluto cry when we get to Nalos' son.

"Son," Nalos greets him, but the boy tilts his head in confusion.

"Do I know you?"

Nalos reaches down and places his hand at the top of the boy's head before stroking it down his forehead. The massive eye closes and then opens when Nalos' fingertips reach the tip of the boy's nose.

"Familiar," the boy says.

"Son," Nalos repeats.

We don't have time for this. We need to get back to Apollo and Eva who are defending themselves against more guards while the massive doors to the menagerie of the stadium begin to open. An arrow comes flying our way. I manage to shift its path with water, but we're running out of that precious commodity, and we're too far from the sea to call for more.

"Nalos, we need to go. Grab him," I shout.

A Griffin swoops out of the sky with its sharp talons at the front ready to grab hold of its victims while allowing the lion hind legs to tear into the flesh.

"Son," Nalos repeats before striking the griffin with his club and killing it.

"Dinner." The boy looks at Nalos.

"Dinner, catch birds." The giant cyclops informs his son.

"Dinner, catch bird."

"Nalos." I spear another guard away with a water arrow. "Please hurry."

Another guard jumps at me. I fixate on the water in his body and drown him from the inside. My powers have also expanded on the island.

"Daddy," the boy finally says.

"Son." Nalos wraps his arms around the boy, and they warmly embrace.

The doors to the stadium are now wide open, and a loud howling can be heard.

"Shit, I hate this dog!" I exclaim, but when the jet black dog emerges, it's not the one I was expecting. It's another chimera—a victim of Pluto's manipulation of nature. The Cerberus that emerges has three heads and so much more. Along it's back are dozens of snakes, their mouths open and fangs bared.

"Nalos, we have to go."

The dog charges for us. Teeth and poisonous fangs, no doubt, ready to impale us. A force field goes up around us, and Eva and Apollo appear at our side.

"What the hell has he done to Cerberus?" I ask Apollo.

"Not sure but we need to get out of here." Apollo grabs Eva's hand. "Nalos, do you have your son?"

"Son, happy." Nalos tucks his boy under his arm.

"We can't," Eva interrupts as I grab her other hand, and Nalos takes her shoulder again.

"Eva now isn't the time to argue. Get us out of here. We have to wait for Jupiter before we can challenge Pluto," Apollo demands.

"Please, for once listen to him, Eva," I plead with her as well.

"But what about the injured children?" Eva's eyes flit to the fallen gladiators on the floor. It's the distraction the beast needs. Cerberus comes at us again. The crowd cheers with excitement when the powerful creature pushes us backward against the wall of the stadium.

"Seriously." Apollo puts his head in his hand.

"We can't leave them. They'll die. Pluto won't look after them."

I know exactly what she's saying. Taking one look at the injured, I know we can't leave them. They didn't ask for this.

"You're the God of Healing, Apollo. With your powers, I can save them."

"Ok, keep together. We need to shuffle toward them. If we can get them behind the shield, we can all teleport out of here together. We won't have long, though, as Pluto and Ambrose will be able to track us down immediately."

"We'll take them to Coventina. She can help," Eva adds.

"Go."

I see Cerberus prepare for another attack. We have only a short distance to move to reach the injured children, but we're under attack from all angles. Guards come at us from the side, and Apollo and Nalos fend them off with sword and club. Eva maintains the shield as best she can, but I can sense she's weakening with every attack from the dog. Water ... I can sense it in the desire of the dog as it bays for blood. It's in its perspiration and the drool forming in its mouth. It's too big an animal for me to kill in the manner I drowned the guards from the inside out, but I can use the water in its sweat and saliva to form arrows. I employ my power and start shooting darts of water into the snake heads. One by one, they fall down dead on the dog's body.

Cerberus slams into the protective shield once again and throws us off balance. We're so tight against the wall. If we take another hit, Eva will have to let the shield down, or it'll squash us against the hard stone of the arena.

"Eva, when I say, let the shield down and throw as many energy balls at the dog as possible." I form a strategy in my head.

"Have you gone insane?" Apollo asks and sends his sword straight through the middle of one of the guards.

"Probably but we aren't going to survive another hit from the dog."

I muster as much power as I can, and bringing the water out of the dog's mouth, I form thousands of tiny arrows.

"Now!" I shout at Eva. She lowers the shield and sends a flurry of energy balls at Cerberus at the same time as I shoot all the arrows into it. It stands there, stunned, trying to figure out what has happened. The snakes on it's back all slump down dead. The dog stumbles. The part that's already dead is destroying the rest of it.

"Get to the children," I call, and we all run at once toward them. Everyone grabs as many hands as we can, and we form a circle.

"Go, Eva," Apollo demands when he completes the hoop.

Cerberus momentarily recovers and bares down on us with all three of its jaws wide open. Its teeth are a fraction away from sheering me in half when we teleport.

APOLLO

One moment, we're in the stadium, and the next, we're back outside the house in the jungle where we started. Eva lets go of my hand. She's shaking and her knees buckle.

"You did good," I tell her, knowing how much the new power she's employing must have cost her in energy, especially having to teleport so many. "I'm proud of you."

Sinking to the grass, she gives me a weak smile.

"Am I supposed to be having a head rush right now?"

"It happens when you overstretch your powers. Your new to moving your atoms around and those of others, but you'll get stronger in time," I explain.

If only I could've teleported too, but for some reason, I'm still blocked.

Nalos sets his son down, watching intently as we check over the other children and wrap up any wounds we can. Pluto and Ambrose will be on our heels. I have no doubt they'll soon hunt us down.

Fontus glances toward the house. "Where's Coventina? I thought she'd come out to investigate by now?"

Finally turning my focus on the building, I absorb the eerie silence. Nothing stirs. None of the usual moaning and groaning emanates from the windows. It feels abandoned.

"Nalo, Eva, stay here and guard the little ones," I order, making my way slowly toward the front door. My lovely demigoddess nods her head, fatigue clear on her beautiful face. The fact she isn't arguing with me, for once, shows just how tired she is.

Fontus falls into step beside me. "Where do you think everyone is?"

"That's what I intend to find out."

Cautiously reaching the entrance, we step over the threshold and listen intently. Again the stillness strikes me as odd. It's too quiet.

Fontus moves to the staircase. "I'll check upstairs."

"Be careful."

He nods sharply at my words.

Concern over his safety has me watching him ascend. I know I need to start trusting them both to take care of themselves though. My two lovers may be many centuries younger than me, but they're both capable of looking after themselves. Believing in their abilities is something I need to do.

The buffet table remains untouched as I enter the dining room. Frowning at the wasted food, my feet take me toward the kitchen. There's no sign of the old woman. A bowl of shelled peas has been left on the counter with a pile of pods beside it waiting to be done. It's as if Coventina had been interrupted. Foreboding crawls up my spine.

Moving toward the back door, I glance out at the rear of the house and freeze. Dark shapes stand stark in the sunlight. It takes me a moment to make them out. Three huge stakes have been hammered into the ground. Hanging from them, hands above their heads nailed into the wood, three crucified bodies dangle lifelessly. A young dark haired woman and two young men. They've been stripped of their clothing, and what's left of their flayed skin, flutters in the breeze like strips of paper. Their abdomens have been sliced open, and their intestines have spilled out beneath them on the grass.

Swallowing down bile, I shuffle away from the view. Ambrose? Was this a punishment for the others because we escaped? Or a warning to us, demonstrating what will happen if we're caught? I dread to think about the fate of Coventina. Eva's heart will break if anything has happened to that old woman. Knowing it's dangerous to remain here, I hurry back to the house.

I find Fontus racing down the stairs his face pale and eyes wide.

"There's no one here ... Did you see the stakes ..."

"Yes," I cut in before he can finish. "We need to move to the beach. Hopefully help will reach us soon ..."

A scream interrupts my words. High and frightened, it comes from somewhere out front. Dashing toward the exit with Fontus behind me, we're in time to see Eva's body jerking, her gaze brimming with pain. Ambrose is standing behind her and catches her as she crumples. White hair rippling as he moves, and a cruel smirk playing across his lips.

Nalos gives a roar of rage. Swinging his club, it meets nothing but air when the evil principal vanishes with Eva in his arms.

EVA

I struggle desperately against Ambrose, but it's to no avail. I can't free myself from his tight grip. I call forth the powers within me, but they're instantly subdued by his magic. He laughs menacingly.

"I'm ready for you, this time. Those aren't your natural powers. They're ones absorbed into your body, so I can control them with preparation. That's my skill." He throws me across the room, and I'm caught by a guard. "Prepare her for examination."

"No!" I shout, and as a second guard grabs hold of me, I try desperately to summon an energy ball, but all I get is the fizzle of the power I had previously. "You don't want to do this. You'll regret it," I spit at Ambrose.

I struggle against the two guards, pulling me toward a hospital examination bed in the corner of the room. I'm shoved onto it, and my legs are unceremoniously pulled apart and strapped into stirrups. Thankfully I'm still wearing the green cotton summer dress I got from Selene and Diana, which keeps me covered.

"I'm not going to regret anything. I love my job. It's the best in the world. I create life and see it develop it's strength and power. I also get my fair share of pussy and ass—I'm not bothered which one." Ambrose comes over to me and strokes his hand down my leg. "Your friend Fontus—I wouldn't mind a share of him. He's got the most perfect dick. It's large and full when erect. He comes beautifully as well even when struggling against me."

My anger erupts. I lean forward and slap him hard in the face. It's the only thing I can do with him in control of my powers.

"You're sick. I'll enjoy seeing you die."

Ambrose clicks his fingers, and my arms are strapped onto the bed as well. I struggle against the bindings.

"Bastard!" I shout at him. He isn't fazed by my outburst though.

He leans down beside my cheek and whispers in my ear, "Struggle all you want. It's what gets me off. You're going to look beautiful decorated in my cum."

The air crackles around us, and Ambrose steps back.

Pluto and Orcus appear in the room.

"I see you brought me a present," Pluto smirks. "I do believe she's a little overdressed for what I have planned for her."

Pluto struts over to me confidently. I desperately try to break the bindings holding me. I summon as much strength as I can, but it's useless. I'm held fast in position, helpless to prevent whatever they're planning. I'll not give up hope, though. I know Apollo and Fontus will never stop until they find me, and if Jupiter comes, then I have a chance. He'll be powerful enough to fight against Pluto's army. I just need to stay calm. Use the strength I've learned from Apollo and Fontus. We're a triad. We brought Apollo back to life with our love. That same love will save me from this. It has to.

Pluto runs a hand over my leg, and I watch as the dress

covering my nakedness from the men in the room disappears. His filthy hand traces over my breasts. I shut my eyes, remembering Fontus' and Apollo's touches and blocking out thoughts of the rough hand currently mauling my flesh. Eventually his hand travels between my thighs, and he melts my underwear away, a rough finger pushes inside me. I'm dry to the touch, and it hurts.

"Please don't do this." I wanted to stay brave, but the plea for mercy leaves my lips before I have a chance to control it.

Pluto comes back up beside me and licks up my face and around to my ear.

"Make sure you cry like that when I'm in your ass, Ambrose is in your mouth, and Orcus is in your pussy. I've heard you like more than one man at a time. We all plan to take advantage of that fact."

He walks away from me laughing, and I fight back the tears forming in my eyes.

Please hurry, Apollo, Fontus, I need you both.

"Examine her. Let's get this over with, and then we can fuck her until she's pregnant. I'm sick of wasting time with this one. I need people with magic, and she has it in abundance right now."

"Of course, master." Ambrose bows to Pluto. The latter takes a seat on a chair in the corner of the room and pulls out his phone to check messages.

"You need a hand?" Orcus questions, a bright smile on his face.

"Yes." Ambrose points to a set of metal instruments on a table. "Pass me the speculum. I need to widen her cervix, so I can get a good look inside. Make sure she's not got any issues that will prevent her from conceiving."

I gulp. As gods we have regular checks to prevent certain

diseases, just like humans, so it's not the first time I've seen a speculum, but this one looks twice the size of the normal ones.

Orcus picks up some lubrication as well.

"Need this?"

Ambrose raises an eyebrow at him.

"What do you think?"

Orcus laughs and throws the lubrication over his shoulder. It almost hits Pluto. He looks up from his phone and sends a cloud of black smoke through the air, whacking it into Orcus' face.

"Careful, Orcus, or you don't get a hole."

"Sorry, sir." Orcus bows to his master in apology.

Pluto returns to his phone as Orcus hands the speculum to Ambrose. Without preparing me, he pushes it inside me and opens it. I breathe deeply at the pain surging through me. My head spins, and I'm on the verge of passing out.

Ambrose bends down in between my legs. He reaches a bony finger out and pushes it inside me through the opening of the speculum.

"Fuck, that's pretty." Orcus licks his lips. I pool saliva in my mouth and spit it at him. He steps forward and hits me in the face. As well as the pain between my legs, I'm now bleeding from a split lip.

"Just you wait until I get inside you." Pluto's right hand man informs me.

"Quiet." Ambrose stands up with a puzzled expression on his face. "Interesting."

"What is it?" Pluto takes his attention away from his phone.

Ambrose comes to my stomach and places his hand on it. He shuts his eyes, and the room falls silent as he concentrates. Pluto puts his phone away and joins us at the examination bed.

"Ambrose?"

Eventually, the principal opens his eyes, and a malevolent grin crosses his face.

"I'm afraid our dicks will not be getting wet in her today. Not unless we take turns in her mouth."

Pluto raises an eyebrow.

"She's pregnant."

"Yes."

Fuck!

I'm pregnant.

"Whose?"

Please don't be Pluto's. Please. Please. Please.

"I'm afraid not yours, my master. It's an interesting pregnancy though. There are two babies."

Shit, I'm expecting twins.

My breath quickens. I'm hyperventilating. All sorts of visions going through my head. Child soldiers like Nalos' son being one of them.

"Two." Pluto rubs his hands together in glee. "A very fertile lady. I like it. We'll keep this one."

"That's the strange thing, my master." Ambrose bows to Pluto. "As far as I can tell, one is Fontus' child, the other Apollo's."

"A child of two demigods, and one of a full god and demigoddess. This couldn't get any better. Grow them quicker. I want the children by the time the sun sets."

"What? No?" Their conversation infiltrates my brain, which had started to fog over at the mention of me being pregnant with twins. "Don't touch me." I'm back struggling against the restraints keeping me bound to the bed despite the fact I know I can't escape them. "You can't do this."

Pluto pushes his weight down on one side of my body to keep it still. Orcus does the same on the other side.

Ambrose reaches out his hand and places it on my stomach. I watch in horror as it starts to grow and swell with the babies inside me.

"Please. No. Don't do this," I cry, but nobody is listening to me.

I focus on Apollo and Fontus, and the powers I have. The only way I can be saved now is to send them every ounce of my strength and magic. I have to save our children. My stomach grows too quickly. They'll take them from me within the hour if I'm not rescued. I already look seven months at least. Shutting my eyes, I will the powers given to me out of my body. I feel them leave in waves of sorrow at my situation. They know they have to return to where they came. It's the only hope for me and my babies. I watch them disappear into the ether as the first wave of labor hits me.

FONTUS

"Eva!" My shout echoes around the clearing, but she's nowhere to be seen. Ambrose has her. Just the thought of what he could be doing to her makes me feel sick.

Apollo's hands are threading in his blond hair—there's a look of desperation on his handsome face. "We have to find her."

"Where the hell would he have taken her?" I question, turning to Nalos.

The cyclops growls, thudding his club against the grassy ground. "Mountain."

Fuck.

Without being able to teleport, it would take us hours to reach them. My stomach clenches in cold dread. Apollo's expression reveals he isn't happy about it either. As he opens his mouth to say something, an explosion from somewhere thunders through the air.

Nalos makes a strange sound in his throat. Grabbing his son to his chest as he crouches over the wounded children protectively.

"Beach!" Apollo hollers, taking off in that direction.

"Stay here. Guard them," I tell the cyclops, who gives me a nod. We race through the clearing and into the trees. I know what he's thinking. Maybe Eva has escaped. She's the strongest one out of us all at the moment.

Reaching the perfect stretch of golden sand and azure water, we halt at what we see.

Chimeras of every shape, size, and description are descending from the tree line. Teeth, claws, wings, scales, scorpion tailed, they're a mismatch of birds and beasts that have been cobbled together. Roaring, screeching, hissing, they flood toward the water.

My attention is caught by the gleam of silver. Emerging from the sea are warriors in armor—wielding swords, they charge forward with a battle cry. Neptune's army. I'd recognize his soldiers anywhere. The god himself rises from the surf on a chariot constructed of thousands of seashells. The great white sharks pulling it, snapping their jaws in anger.

"The cavalry's here!" I tell Apollo, slapping him on the shoulder.

"Don't let them scratch you with their claws," he bellows as monsters and men clash.

Hurrying close, we avoid the fighters as they spear the creatures and hack at them with swords. Grabbing Apollo's arm, I direct him toward the sea god as he dismounts his ride.

"My, King." Dropping to my knee before him, I bow my head. "Thank the stars you've arrived."

"Where's my daughter, Fontus?" Neptune's voice is deep and haughty.

Raising my head, I find him eyeing the man beside me with suspicion. Apollo stands tall with a hint of the arrogance I've seen in him before.

"One of Pluto's minions has her," Apollo responds.

"You should have informed Jupiter the second you heard

of this place," my King scolds the younger god. "Coming here alone was head strong and foolish. You endangered not only yourself but my daughter and her betrothed."

Getting to my feet, I blink up at him in confusion at the last word. "Betrothed?"

Neptune nods, his steely gaze sweeping the fighting going on around us. "I've allowed Eva to roam freely for too long. This is the last straw. She'll marry you and end her wild ways. They'll be no more sneaking off for adventures."

Marriage to Eva? My heart swells with the thought. Glancing at the god beside me, it falters when I see his scowl. I can't wed her unless Apollo's part of our marriage as well. It's the three of us together or not at all. However, with the glare Neptune is currently directing at Apollo, I'm not sure it's the best time to inform him of that.

"Apollo!"

The female voice has us all turning to look at the blonde woman who's stalking toward us. Crossbow in her hands, she's taking out the enemy with a deadly aim. The resemblance is so uncanny I know this must be Apollo's twin, Diana.

Apollo sighs. "What are *you* doing here?"

"Father sent me," she informs him, flicking some blonde hair insolently out of her face. "You managed to get yourself killed, and you fucked up. I'm here to clean up your mess."

"I did not fuck up," he growls through clenched teeth.

Diana rolls her blue eyes. "Sure you didn't."

"Can you teleport?"

She frowns at his question. "Of course, I can."

Apollo slices me a look. "Good we need you to ..."

He never gets to finish his sentence. Immense power... it hits us both like a freight train, sending us across the beach, into the surf, and onto our asses. Gasping for breath, I feel it overwhelm me.

Eva.

It's laced with her being, threaded through with desperation and sorrow.

APOLLO

Warm sea water drenches my shorts and legs. Ignoring the discomfort, I focus on the fact my powers have returned. They course through my body, stronger than ever, and now they're mixed with Eva's essence. I can taste my little sea goddess on my tongue. Her smell invades my senses along with her fear. Hooking onto that essence of her, I know I can find her.

"We need to go now," I shout to Fontus.

He's already on his feet. From his expression, he's just experienced the same thing I have. Clamping my hand down on his arm, I don't realize someone else has also grabbed hold of me until I teleport.

Materializing in a dimly lit corridor, I release my lover to turn angrily on my pain in the ass twin. "You should have stayed on the bloody beach."

"Oh, *please.*" Cradling her cross bow in the crook of her arm, Diana gives me a sardonic look. "Like I'm going to let you out of my sight, so you can die again."

Grinding my teeth, I swallow down my retort. Eva is more important than trading insults with my sister right now.

A high pitched wail of someone in distress breaks the sudden silence.

"Eva," Fontus mutters.

"Wait you idiots! It could be a trap," Diana calls after us as we break into a run.

The thought of losing our feisty female drives any thought of caution from my head. Bursting through a doorway, the sight that greets us is surreal. Ambrose is standing between Eva's spread thighs. Her feet are strapped into stirrups. The huge swell of her pregnant stomach is unmistakable as she strains and arches in the rigors of childbirth.

Eyes wide and glued to the ceiling, her face twists in pain, and she screams.

A new sound joins in. The sharp cry of a newborn.

Dumbstruck, all I can do is watch as Ambrose lifts the baby, its tiny feet kicking, and its mouth wide open as it yells. How is it possible? Bouncing a look at Fontus, he's standing beside me with his mouth gaping.

"Get out of the way." A hand shoves me aside. The next thing I know, my sister is storming the room with her weapon ready.

"Orcus," she says as Pluto's second in command jerks his head our way, and his eyes widen.

A blur comes at us, and Diana is thrown sideways into the wall as the hulking monster of a god barrels into her. I'm in time to see Ambrose wrapping the newborn in a towel before handing it off to Pluto, who's been hiding in the shadows.

He gives me an evil smirk as he and Ambrose vanish.

A fist ploughs into my face, scattering my thoughts. The second blow doesn't reach me as Fontus deflects it. Bringing my arm around, I punch Orcus in the nose and hearing it crack brings me some satisfaction.

"Get out of the way!" Diana shouts.

Pushing Fontus sideways, we narrowly miss the arrow as it streaks through the air to embed in Orcus' shoulder.

"Help me!"

Eva's distressed sob has me darting to her side. "It's ok. We'll get the baby back."

Pressing a kiss to her cheek, I wipe her damp forehead.

"Orcus has vanished," Fontus tells me as he joins us.

Still clutching her crossbow and scanning the room for threats, my sister moves to the foot of the bed. Her countenance pales when she looks toward Eva. "Oh crap!"

At the same moment my sister speaks, Eva tenses, her whole frame twisting as a shriek works its way out of her throat. Alarmed, I grab her hand, which has been secured to the bed, and hold it tightly. "We're going to get you out of here."

"We've got a bigger problem than that," Diana growls, her gaze glued between my lover's spread legs. "Do either of you know how to deliver a baby?"

Fontus tilts his head in confusion. "What the hell are you talking about? Pluto just stole her baby."

"Well then who wants to explain to me why I can see a head trying to squeeze itself out of your girlfriend's sex hole?" she snaps back.

EVA

My overstretched and bruised body prepares to bear down again and push a second baby from it. I don't need to see it to know that this child will be Fontus'. The first was greeted with great delight from Pluto and Ambrose. A powerful child born of a full god and a demigoddess. I didn't even get to see my son before they took him away. He's just what they need to grow their army.

"You're a woman. Help her," Apollo orders his sister.

"I may be a woman, but I've no experience in this kind of thing. I don't know what to do," Diana responds while backing away from me.

The urge to push is overwhelming. I need to get this baby out of me.

"Stop fucking arguing and do something," I scream at all three of them.

They look at me, shocked. Apollo's and Fontus' jaws drop open.

A commotion comes from outside.

"I'll deal with that," Diana says before any of the others can move, and she disappears out through the door.

"It's coming out farther." Fontus looks down between my legs. "Apollo?"

"Eva what the hell is going on? How are you giving birth?" Apollo asks.

I lie my head back on the bed.

"Ask me your questions after you get this thing out of me!" I shout through gritted teeth.

"Ok." Apollo seems to snap out of his shock. The healing side to his powers come to the forefront. He bends down in between my legs, and I feel him guiding the baby's head out of me when I push again. Everything is burning, but Fontus comes to my side and holds my hand. I feel a wave of comfort wash over me, and it's better than any drug that could be administered.

I listen to Apollo as he guides me through the process of giving birth again. The baby, another boy, is delivered onto my chest. All three of us sit in silence as the newborn latches onto my exposed breast and takes his first nourishment from me.

"Congratulations." Apollo is the first to speak. He looks down at the ground, an expression of sadness on his face. It's obvious from the dark hair that the baby is Fontus'. "I'll finish tidying you up down below."

"Wait." I reach out to him. "I have two children. This one's father is Fontus, but the other baby is yours."

A tear falls down my cheek at the enormity of what has just happened. I'm a mother. The magic of the island is overwhelming. I want to sleep.

"How is that possible?" Apollo looks confused. "I don't understand."

"The island. It's the only explanation." My voice catches in my throat, and I let out a sob. "They took our son, Apollo."

The door to the room I'm in opens, and my father's face

appears in it. I've never been so happy to see him, but when he sees the position I'm in, his face turns white.

"Somebody care to explain what's going on?" He comes over to the bed. My arms are still bound to it. Fontus releases them and helps me to sit up. Apollo places a hand over my lower regions and heals them of the pain of giving birth. He's still not said anything about being a father.

Fontus takes the baby from me and shows him to my father.

"I'd like to introduce you to your grandson, my king."

My father's eyes go wide.

"How? You've only been missing a short time. It's not possible."

"Magic, Father. It's all part of Pluto's breeding plan." I reach down the bed and take Apollo's hand. "This isn't your only grandson. Pluto took the child Apollo and I have together."

"Together?" My father spits out.

"Yes. We're all together," I inform him. He looks between the three of us and then bursts out laughing. "Only my daughter! Didn't think there would ever be one man alone who could handle you."

The air crackles around us.

"Oh, shit," Apollo finally speaks. "Care to explain that to my father."

A lightning bolt shoots through the sky, and Jupiter appears in the room, his feet making scorch marks on the floor.

"Explain what to me?" Jupiter questions.

I'm terrified of the look on his face. He's livid. I sit up straighter. Fontus waves a hand over me, and I'm wearing my summer dress again.

Neptune laughs.

"Hi, Grandad," my father teases his powerful counterpart and best friend.

"Grandad? Venus has had her baby?" Jupiter looks confused. My second born, nestled in Fontus' arms, chooses that moment to cry.

"Whose baby is this?" Jupiter asks.

"Mine, sir," Fontus replies. "And Eva's."

"Then why am I a grandad?" Jupiter rubs his hand over his head.

"Because she had one with Apollo at the same time." My father claps his hand on Jupiter's back. "We share a grandchild."

"We what? How?"

"Magic, Father," Apollo admits. I can still feel the anger and sadness radiating off him.

"Where is it?" Jupiter asks, looking around the room for the other child.

"Pluto has him," I admit.

"What?" Jupiter spits at me. "Apollo?"

"He's taken him for his army."

The room starts to crackle again. Anger rolls off Jupiter in waves, and the baby I have with Fontus cries louder.

"Enough," Jupiter roars. He grabs Apollo by the arm, and they both disappear before we have a chance to stop them.

FONTUS

I can't imagine what is going through Apollo's mind as I look down at my son in my arms. It's a shock, but one I couldn't be happier about. I see Eva mixed with myself in the baby nestling down as I sway him gently back to sleep.

Eva's scream of anguish when Apollo disappears jolts my boy awake again. He cries for his mother, so I hand him over. Neptune strokes at his new grandson's head.

"Find Coventina," Eva orders me. "Think of her, and you'll be taken to her."

"Why?" I'm slightly worried why Eva wants the old lady.

"Because we're going to need her to look after the baby while we go get Apollo and our other son."

"No," Neptune and I both say at the same time.

Eva jumps off the bed with the baby tucked in her arms. He's quietened down now and is finally sleeping. My beautiful water goddess doesn't look like a woman who gave birth moments ago.

"I'm warning you both. Don't try telling me no. Jupiter has taken one of the men I love down to Hell where Pluto already has one of my babies. I'm going after them, and you're going to give me some of your powers in case I need them. Eva hands the baby to her father and places her hand on my shoulder. I feel a portion of the new magic within me swell and flow from me back to her. She tests it out by sending a small wave of power at me. It knocks me flat on my ass again.

"Damn, I love you in this mood." I chuckle and get back up to my feet.

"I'll go get Coventina."

"You're kidding, right?" my king questions.

"I'll let you argue with Eva while I fetch her friend," I tell him before thinking of the helpful old lady and disappearing from the room. I instantly miss my son when I do.

When I come back to my senses after the teleportation, I find myself on the edge of a volcano. Coventina is lying on the ground. She's strapped down and the bubbling lava is flowing toward her.

"Shit." Moving quickly, I burn away the rope holding her down, and scooping her up into my arms, I teleport us farther down the mountain.

"What happened?" I question, checking her for injuries

"Pluto. He knows the island is compromised. He's moved all the remaining children off it. He started the volcano erupting to destroy the evidence of what he's been doing." She looks to see the progression of the lava. It's now flowing directly over the place where she'd been lying moments earlier. "That was to be my punishment for helping you."

"How long do we have?"

The earth suddenly shakes underneath us, and a stream of lava erupts from the volcano.

"We need to leave now," she tells me.

The injured children and Nalos are still at the house. We have to save them. I take Coventina's hand and teleport with her back to Eva.

When we arrive, Eva looks at me wide eyed.

"What's going on, Fontus? We felt an earthquake," she asks.

"There's a volcano erupting. It's going to cover the island in a matter of minutes. We need to get everyone off.

"I'll get my men off. But we can't take everyone into the sea. They won't be able to breathe underwater or swim that far," Neptune says.

"We need to teleport them."

Diana suddenly appears back in the room.

"We've a problem?"

"Volcano?" I inquire.

"How did you know?" She looks at Neptune, who still has the baby in his arms. "Is that the baby?"

"Yes." Eva takes him from her father and hands our son to Coventina.

"The other one?" The old lady asks.

"How do you know?" Eva's stunned.

"Magic."

We all shake our heads. The island trembles again.

"Diana, take Coventina and the baby to your father's house. I know where it is, so Fontus and I will bring the others there as soon as we can."

"I don't think my father's going to like that. Apollo, tell her?" Diana looks around the room. "Er, where's my brother?"

"See, this is what happens when you chicken out on watching someone giving birth. You miss the moment your father takes your brother to Hell with him," Eva responds.

"Crap."

The building shakes, and the walls around us start to crumble."

"Go," Eva shouts, and we all disappear to our respective duties.

I land with my lover at the house where Nalos is sitting outside with the children. He's telling them a story, but I can tell from the ashen color of their faces they are terrified of what is happening on the island.

"Do you think we can take them all at the same time? You brought them here with full power. We only have half now," I ask Eva.

I'm worried we won't have the strength to achieve this in one go, and I'm not sure we'll get another chance to come back.

A loud bang sounds, and I turn around to see a stream of volcanic rocks heading for us.

"Don't know, but we're about to find out. Everyone hold hands," Eva shouts. We all obey immediately and teleport out of there seconds before the rocks land exactly where we were sitting.

When I open my eyes, we're in Jupiter's opulent mansion. I've been here once before for a party, but at the moment, it looks more like a refugee camp. Juno, the wife of the King of the Gods, starts running around checking the children. A man and heavily pregnant woman assist her. I recognize the man as Mars, the God of War.

Eva instantly goes to our son and checks on him. I follow her, feeling weary but also worrying about Apollo. My instincts tell me he's suffering with the fear of losing our other child—his biological son. I hope there isn't any other reason for his anguish.

"Where's my brother?" Mars comes up to us.

"You're father teleported them to go after our other baby," Eva replies. She looks exhausted. It must be so hard for her, not being able to care for her other son the way she is for this one.

Eva kisses the top of our baby's head and stands up.

"You ready?" she asks.

"You need to rest." I don't like the idea forming in her head.

"Not until I have Apollo and our other child with me."

Venus comes over, her hand resting on her stomach and whispers to Mars, "She reminds me of me."

"A pain in the ass." Mars raises an eyebrow at her.

"No, stubborn and determined. Go with them. Be careful." Venus kisses her husband and turns back to tend the children.

"Well." Eva puts her hands on her hips. Her lips pout together, daring me to deny her the right to come and join the fight with us.

"Ok." We all join hands. At the last minute, Diana puts her hand in as well.

"Think of Apollo," I say, and we all disappear down to the gates of Hell.

APOLLO

My ears still ring with Eva's cry as I vanish with my father. The sight of the baby feeding from her breast remains vivid in my mind. A son. I have a child, and Pluto has his hands on him. The fear at what the God of the Underworld might do to him almost cripples me. We need to get him back. I'd never forgive myself if anything happened to him, and I wouldn't expect Eva to either. I know Fontus will keep both her and his own son safe.

We materialize in an opulent hall with thick, black pillars in obsidian, stretching the length of the spacious room. Armed soldiers line the walls, spears at the ready to attack us.

Jupiter, my father, King of the Gods, straightens to his full height beside me, his silver threaded eyebrows dipping in a fearsome scowl.

"Pluto! Show yourself, you coward."

The men encircling us move uneasily but are yet to attack. Pluto's minions. Not full gods but I sense some of them have traces of the divine in their blood. More of the children he's been breeding? It sickens me to think how many innocents he's corrupted over the centuries right under our noses.

Orcus skulks out of the shadows at the end of the room near to a throne of gold and jewels.

"You do not have permission to be here," he remarks.

Jupiter snorts. "Like that's ever stopped your master before. Why should I give him a courtesy he doesn't afford me?"

It's all I can do to hold myself back from running at the ugly brute and demanding my son.

Orcus' eyes narrow on my face, and his lips curve up as though he can sense my tightly leashed anger. "Pluto's not available to see you."

"I don't give a fuck," I spit, my temper finally slipping. "I want my son returned to me now."

Orcus laughs. "Yours? The child produced by that little demigoddess is Pluto's."

My breath seizes in my chest, and I shake my head in disbelief. "Bullshit, I don't believe you."

"We're not leaving until we see the baby." My father's tone is edged with command. When I glance his way, I see his expression is firm with determination. "The mother insists it's Apollo's, and even if it isn't, Pluto had no right to take it from her arms."

What if Eva was wrong? What if the God of the Under-world is the father? He'd raped her more than once. How can she be so sure that it's mine? She has Fontus and their son now. She's betrothed to him—she won't want me. Small insidious whispers. Ones that work their way through my thoughts.

"Stay strong, Apollo," my father murmurs, garnering my attention. "This place will use your inner doubts and fears against you. Do not fall prey to its influence, or Pluto will take advantage of it."

Manipulation and mind games. Something the evil god is known for. I should have realized the very air in his domain would ooze with it.

Orcus motions to one of the guards. Whispering in the man's ear, he sends him off with a message. A tense silence follows. My gaze sweeps over our captors, and I make a mental note of ways to disarm them. Electricity tingles in the air around my father. From his rigid stance, he's clearly ready to fry anyone stupid enough to attempt to bring us down.

"What is it you want?" Pluto questions as he steps into the room, his long legs gliding across the floor as if he doesn't have a care in the world. There's no sign of the baby or Ambrose.

"You took something that doesn't belong to you," I growl. "You've held people captive to breed them like animals on a cloaked magical island, and you've used their children to fill the ranks of your unholy army. You must pay for your crimes."

Easing down onto his throne, he smirks. "What island? You have no proof if it doesn't exist."

"Only because you destroyed it," I reply, my rage boiling just beneath the surface of my outer calm. "I saw what you did there. We have survivors. An old woman, a cyclops, and some of the children you were using."

"Ah, the senile hag. Her mind is gone, and she doesn't know the truth from a lie. The cyclops is an enemy, who'd say anything to get me into trouble, and as for the brats … foundlings without parents that I look under my wing out of the goodness of my heart."

My father snorts beside me. "Well we all know your lying about that."

Taking a step toward him, I push the tip of one of the spears aimed at me to the side with my finger. "Cut the crap, Pluto, and give me my son.

The cool façade he's been portraying shatters as his lips curl up in an unpleasant sneer. "He belongs to me now. If you're so desperate for another bastard, why don't you go knock up that sea goddess again. I'm sure it won't take much to get her to spread her legs for you a second time."

A red haze rises in front of my eyes. Before I even realize what I'm doing, I toss the soldiers aside. With all my centuries of training and fighting, I've become hardened over time—they don't stand a chance against me as I fight to get my hands on the monster sitting on his throne.

The air crackles as my father lets loose a couple of lightning bolts, clearing the way before me. Charging forward, I disarm a guard to my left, claiming his spear as I smack him onto his ass. Raising it, I hurl it with precision. Before it can hit Pluto in the chest, Orcus plucks it out of the air.

Pluto's chuckle is sinister. "Hmmm a hot head just like your brother Mars."

"Apollo, wait!" my father bellows, but I don't heed his words.

When the God of the Underworld rises and dashes for a door, I follow with every intention of beating the whereabouts of my son out of his slimy hide. Running along a corridor, he vanishes through another door. With my mind focused on catching him and making him pay, I don't stop to consider it might be a trap.

Pain erupts through my body the second I pass the threshold. Screaming out in agony, it blinds me as my knees hit the floor. Jerking, spasming, I fall sideways, gasping for breath.

"Foolish boy," Pluto taunts. "How simple it was to lead you away. You made my plan as easy as taking candy from a baby."

Ambrose grins, his powers still arcing through every one of my nerve endings and paralyzing me in place. In the crook of his other arm, a baby lies sleeping, swaddled in a towel.

"Give ... give me ... my son," I demand, struggling to speak. I'm unable to move and overwhelmed.

Crouching down, Pluto runs a bony finger along my jaw. "Oh, don't worry. You'll have plenty more. We're going to extract your sperm and implant it into the other demigoddesses we have detained."

More of his camps. More innocent lives suffering at his hands. How many? How many does he have? The thought of him forcing females to bear my children to become his slaves sends my stomach twisting with bile. I can't let this happen. I'd rather die than allow it even if it means being parted from Fontus and Eva forever.

Eyes glazed and unfocused, I stare up into his evil face. "No."

"It won't take long. Ambrose is very good at what he does. By the time your father comes racing to your rescue, I'll already have what I need."

The principal hands the sleeping boy into the arms of a guard before collecting a worn leather bag from a table. "Strip him. We'll do it on the floor."

I'm grabbed roughly and turned onto my back. Swearing and thrashing about, my feeble attempts to smack away the intrusive hands that strip me of my shorts do little good. Pain builds inside me every time I call on my powers.

I'm in a choke hold—it's keeping me in check and preventing me from fighting. Fury collides with impotent helplessness. I'm Apollo. A fucking god, and this son of a bitch is blocking me.

Pluto chuckles above me. "I'll let you into a little secret. Ambrose isn't just the principal of my camps. He's also one of the first children produced from them. That old hag that helped you. She's his mother."

Before I can even process Pluto's words, I see the white-haired bastard has a needle in his hand. "I'm not going to lie this will hurt you a lot more than it will me, but I'll enjoy hearing your screams," Ambrose says and grins, his eyes gleaming with sadistic pleasure.

EVA

I'm not particularly looking forward to visiting Hell again, but I know it's the only way we're going to be able to find Apollo and my other son. I'll not let Pluto win. This time, I'm ready for him.

My mind is full of thoughts of my blond-haired lover as we land down in the depths of the Underworld. I expected a fight to be ensuing but not the scene I see before me. Apollo is laid bare on the floor while Ambrose strokes my lover's dick.

"No!" Fontus shouts toward them, and the anguish in his voice tells me this is what the principal did to him as well. My brown-haired lover forms energy balls in his hand and in fury launches them at the principal, but they are all deflected.

"For fuck's sake, I thought we had guards at the gates of Hell. Are they just letting anyone in now?" Pluto curses and makes his way toward one of the guards. It's then I see my child in the man's arms.

Mars rushes for Pluto, the God of War having his own score to settle with the God of the Underworld, but my focus is purely on my baby.

"Fontus, Diana, help Apollo," I order, taking charge. Diana starts to argue with me, but when she sees me heading for my son, she shuts her mouth tightly and heads for Ambrose with Fontus.

"Guards!" Pluto shouts.

Mars transforms into his warrior state. A massive spear appears in his hand, and he charges at the God of the Underworld.

"Did you not learn your lesson last time?" Mars roars.

"Did you?" Pluto snarls back and swipes the God of War into a wall.

Mars instantly comes back at Pluto, and I realize he's distracting the God of the Underworld to prevent him disappearing with my child again. I take my opportunity and descend upon the guard holding my son. He tries to run, but I block his path, and he's left stranded in the room.

"Anyone ever told you not to get between a mother and her child? It's a certain path to death," I sneer.

Two additional guards appear in front of him, and shots are fired directly at me. I sense the water of the river of pain nearby, which is just what I need. I call it forth and dispel the shots back at the guards as well as the water. It flows into their ears, nostrils, any orifice it can find, and I watch as the pain starts. Death stalks them with untold agony.

A few moments later, the guards are dead, and the one behind them holds my son closer to his chest, more in fear than in menace.

"Give him back," I demand, leaving little leeway as to my intention.

"Watch out!" Diana shouts from behind me, and I spin around in time to see Orcus heading for me with a sword drawn.

"Get out of here," he orders the guard, but I make it

impossible for the man to move by using yet more water to anchor his feet to the ground.

"He's going nowhere," I say through gritted teeth. A guttural growl of fury comes from deep within my stomach. I'm a woman possessed now. I've had enough. I want to be at home with Apollo, Fontus, and our sons. I'm done with this shit. You can only push me so far. I thought they'd hit those buttons already, but no, now I'm really pissed. Seriously pissed off and Orcus is going to experience the brunt of it.

Summoning up a mixture of my water abilities and Apollo's strength with arrows, I hit Orcus with as much power as I can muster. He staggers backward, his mouth open in shock. Hundreds of arrows stick out of his body, and water from the river of pain seeps into the holes. He starts screaming in agony before he shuts his eyes, and all his injuries disappear.

"You aren't the only one with magic, little princess," he chuckles before calling forth black mists that swirl around my body, pulling tighter and tighter to restrict my breathing. I'm too strong and disintegrate them to nothing before they can reach my face and completely stop me breathing.

"Yes, but as I said to those idiots lying on the floor, don't get between a mother and her child. Your scheme with Pluto is at an end. It's discovered and will be destroyed, no matter how much you try to hide the evidence. I will personally swim to every island and free every single woman and man you hold captive, and all who've been raped by you and Pluto. I'll give them sanctuary and hope, not the magical lust that you seem to thrive on. But my greatest gift to them will be ensuring that you'll never again be able to treat a woman the way you did me and the others.

Orcus raises a skeptical eyebrow at me.

"Confidence leads to a downfall."

I smirk.

"Not in this case."

Before Orcus has a chance to act, I call forth the water again and have it travel up his legs. He tries to shake it away before magically trying to expel it from his body. My intentions are too strong though, and I wrap it around his dick, which is hanging loose in his pants.

"Stop!" he shouts, but I have no intention of doing so. With a click of my fingers, the water pulls tightly, and like a shard of the sharpest glass, it severs his cock from his body.

Orcus scream out in pain, and then in a flash, he disappears from the room.

Turning back to the guard, I lick my lips. A new found appreciation for revenge courses through my body.

"I believe you have something of mine, and I want it back."

The guard takes one look at me and then at Pluto, who's in deep battle with Mars. The two of them are paying little attention to us as they trade blow after blow. I should want to destroy Pluto for what he's done to me. I should be the one fighting him, but all I want is my child. The guy recognizes he'd be stupid to mess with me, and he shoots his arms out toward me with my son held in them.

"T-Take him," the man stutters. I step forward, and keeping my attention on both the man and the baby to prevent any last minute tricks, I take my other son into my arms for the first time. He's the spitting image of Apollo: handsome with blond hair and blue eyes. My heart melts for a second time that day. The guard prepares to scamper from the room, but he's involved in this plan, and I can't let him get away. He may be a child of this project, but he's too old to be changed back now, his mind has been broken by Pluto's ploy to create an army. I'm kind and end his life with a quick twist of magic to his neck. He doesn't need to suffer like Orcus is at this very moment.

Nestling the baby into my chest, I smile down at him.

"Time to get your daddies and go home."

FONTUS

Chapter Thirty Nine

"Careful now." Ambrose smirks. "You wouldn't want to hit your lover now, would you?"

The energy ball I'm aiming at him in my palm wavers. Apollo is still on the floor locked in agony under the principal's influence. The thought of hurting him accidentally holds me back.

"Just fucking do it, Fontus," the blond god snaps, his muscled body shuddering with his suffering. There's enough steel in his voice to make my uncertainty ebb.

Ambrose kicks him in the ribs to silence him.

I toss the energy ball at his white-haired head, but he raises his hand at the last moment and deflects it.

"You're no match for me alone, demigod," Ambrose boasts with a sneer.

"Who said anything about him being alone?" Diana steps up beside me, letting loose some arrows from her crossbow. Agile and swift, the principal moves his body in a blur, managing to dodge all but one of her deadly arrows. The one that found its target has buried itself in his shoulder. A hiss of pain escapes from his lips.

It's enough of a distraction for Apollo to break free. Rolling away from Ambrose, he sends an energy ball crashing into the principal's back. His slender frame is thrown across the room to crash into the wall with a crack.

"Put your junk away," Diana snaps at her brother, her eyes looking anywhere but his dick.

Snatching up his shorts, he quickly stabs his legs through the holes. "It's not like I had a choice. I was being molested for my sperm!"

Nausea burns in my throat at the knowledge. The same treatment I'd suffered at Ambrose's hands sends echoes of disgust roiling through me. I want to punish him for what he's done. Make him feel as helpless as I'd felt when he'd been forcing me to orgasm with his bony hand.

"Easy, Fontus," Apollo tells me, gently reaching my side and squeezing my shoulder. "He'll pay for all his crimes. I promise."

I can see Diana to the left of us, engaging with enemy reinforcements. We're still knee deep in the underbelly of Hell, and I know eventually even we will be overrun by Pluto's forces. We need to leave. Get out before the God of the Underworld overpowers us and has us all at his mercy.

"Watch out!"

Diana's warning comes just in time. Pushing Apollo aside, the spear meant for his back meets empty air instead. Baring his teeth, his gaze wild, Ambrose thrusts the weapon toward me this time, Diana's arrow is still buried deep in his shoulder. Leaping backward, the razor edged tip slices through my skin, leaving a crimson line in its wake.

My blond lover bellows in anger. Charging the slender male, Apollo ploughs his shoulder into Ambrose's chest. The force is enough to take the principal off his feet and have him landing on his ass. The spear flies out of his grip.

"Not so much fun when those your picking on have their

powers," Apollo snarls at the white-haired male. When Ambrose goes to raise his hand, Apollo smashes it into the wall, preventing him from using his powers to inflict pain.

The sickening sound of bones shattering gives me a sliver of satisfaction. After all the misery and torture he's dished out over god-knows-how-long, he deserves to feel it returned to him tenfold.

Ambrose glowers. "You think you've won, but this is nothing but a battle. The war is far from over. We have islands in places not even you will find. You've barely scratched the surface of our setup. It's been running for centuries right under your ignorant noses."

Scooping up the weapon he's dropped, I aim the deadly pointed end at his face. "We found one, so there's nothing stopping us from finding the others. You won't be around to see the end result, but know this, everything you have created will come to nothing but ruin."

"Don't." Apollo clutches my wrist, preventing me from ending the vile creature. "He could be useful to us. We could interrogate him for the locations we need."

The spear wavers in my grip. A need for vengeance crashes through me, but Apollo's words stop me from killing the monster still slumped on the floor. Across the room, I see Eva protectively cradling the child we've come for as she watches us in silence.

Although everything in me wants to kill Ambrose, I know it can't end this way. Apollo is right. The information we can torture out of him is far too valuable. Innocent lives are at stake. It's our duty to find them and bring them home safely.

Ambrose uses the distraction, and with a wave of his one good hand, he sends pain crashing through me. Agony sears my nerve endings, and my knees meet the marble floor—the weapon in my hand is forgotten. I hear the cries of everyone in the room, mirroring my own. With black spots dancing before my vision, though, I'm blinded to anything else.

Fingers fist my hair, tilting my head upward, the force behind them almost ripping the strands from my scalp.

"I'll be waiting to take your sons when you least expect it." The principal hisses against my ear, his breath hot against my cheek. "It will be at the moment when you are the happiest and most unaware. Everything you love will die at my hands. Your children will become devoted followers of Pluto, and the world you love so much will be consumed in flames."

Panic tightens my chest. Just when I think I can bear it no longer, I'm suddenly free of the energy holding me prisoner. Apollo is on his feet beside me, his very being pulsing with music. I've never seen anything like it. Bathing him in a golden light, it's bright and as warm as the rays of the sun. I watch as it flows out of him in a mighty wave, roaring into Ambrose with such strength it's like Apollo's created a tsunami of sound.

Ambrose screams as he's thrown clear across the room and flies into the wall beside the doorway, blood pouring from his ears and nose. Crumpling to the ground, he lays in an unconscious heap.

"Fuck it, just end him, Fontus," Apollo instructs, retrieving the spear and handing it to me. "No one threatens our family and lives. I won't risk having him come after our little ones again."

Eva nods. "We'll find the other islands another way. He can't be allowed to slither away. We must all agree to pass judgement here and now."

I don't even hesitate. Powering my arm back, I aim

straight at the evil man's heart, and I let the spear loose. Unfortunately, it doesn't have a chance to meet its mark. Pluto appears out of nowhere, a scowl on his sharp features, and with a flick of his hand, he sends the missile tumbling uselessly to the floor.

"I have use for my principal yet. You may have rescued your child, but you will not take Ambrose from me when his work is not yet completed," he snaps, glaring as Mars comes to stand beside Apollo.

The God of War plants his hands on his hips, looking no less intimidating than before. "Give it up, Pluto. You're never going to win."

"We have a problem," Diana hollers as Jupiter comes to join our group. "There's a shit load more soldiers on the way. I'm not talking about the ones he's bred. These things are monstrous and crawling up from the depths of the Underworld."

Pluto sneers, "Not even you will be able to fight off all my demons."

"Time to go!" Jupiter herds us all into a group.

Energy surrounds us, and in the next moment, I take a breath of warm Roman air.

APOLLO

Chapter Forty

Returning to my father's villa in Rome, we find the rescued children well-tended to. Even Nalos and his son have been made welcome. Finding them a new home will be a priority as we can't have a couple of cyclopes roaming the human world. Mankind believe us to be nothing but myths and legends, and like our ongoing war with Pluto, keeping it that way is essential to stop them from panicking.

"They've lost their home," Eva murmurs sadly, hugging our child close to her breast.

Brushing a kiss to her forehead, I smile. "We'll find them somewhere new to live. Diana has a house far up in the Dolomites. Humans rarely climb to that height, and I'm sure she has plenty of room with her menagerie of animals and beasts."

I feel Eva's sadness as if it's my own. The island is gone. All its magic and the creatures that lived on it have been destroyed by the anger of the volcano that Pluto unleashed. In one way, I'm relieved, but in another, I mourn the loss. Nalos helped us on the island. We won't abandon him now. Whatever he needs we'll provide, and we'll welcome him and his boy into our expanding family.

My twin's blue eyes narrow dangerously in my direction.

"Now hold on just a minute, you can't decide who I have on my mountains."

"It's the perfect place for them. There are plenty of peaks untouched by man where they can make a fresh start," Jupiter responds.

Our father's not looking any worse for wear after his fight with Pluto's men. In fact, there's a new spring in his step and a sparkle in his eye. After their previous disastrous meeting, it looks like he's finally regained his confidence.

Diana huffs, palming her crossbow. She's always been the odd one out. She finds more comfort in animals and mystical creatures than she does with the rest of us. I know she'll eventually see it our way and let them stay with her. Under all her prickly warrior exterior, she truly has a big heart for those in need.

The cry of a baby distracts me. Coventina appears in the room with a warm smile on her wrinkled face as she carries our other twin toward us. Looking a little disheveled, Fontus hurries to meet her, taking the fussing baby into his arms.

"He's been fine," the old woman assures him. "Nothing I couldn't handle."

Eva gives her a warm smile. "Thank you, Coventina. We owe you so much for helping us on the island."

Coventina waves her words away. "You are the ones who helped me. I thought I'd never escape. Now, finally, I can return to the sea. It's something I've yearned to do for so long."

I stare down at the child in Eva's arms that looks so much like me. It makes tears mist in my eyes. I never gave a thought to ever becoming a father, yet here I am with two sons. My gaze takes in Fontus and our second boy child in his arms. The look of awe he wears, I know, is mirrored in my expression. We're bound together even more, and these ties can never be broken. They're locked in my heart, and I vow never to let them leave it.

"He looks just like you," my father points out. "Here I was thinking Venus would produce our second grandchild. You've beaten Mars to it."

I grin at my older brother, who has an arm curved around his heavily pregnant wife. "I guess you're not the best at everything after all."

Mars raises an eyebrow. "Don't get cocky, little brother."

Venus laughs, poking him in the ribs. "Don't worry, we'll have our hands full soon enough."

"I already have a son," he points out, giving me a smug stare. "You'll have to get used to changing diapers and night feeds. Let's see how bigheaded you are about it then!"

Wrinkling my nose, I realize he's right. My bachelor life has ended in the blink of an eye. I have responsibilities now to my mates and our babies. It should be a terrifying thought, but it's not. Instead, contentment washes through me. Glancing at my lovers, I find them watching me closely.

"We better get some practice in then," I tell Fontus. "We can't expect Eva to cope alone."

"That was never going to happen," he points out, his attention proudly focused on the boy in his arms. "She'd kick our asses if we slacked."

That's true. She might be submissive in bed, but our little sea goddess knows how to hold her own. I'm more than proud of her. Down in the Underworld, she showed us just how strong she can be. With our triad and powers entwined, we're stronger now and unstoppable.

Laughing, Eva offers Jupiter his grandson. Carefully scooping up the baby, who's now awake, he cradles the gurgling infant in his arms. They stare at each other, the elder god making noises and pulling faces.

"Have you named them yet?" Coventina asks, watching over them with a motherly eye.

Eva, Fontus, and I share a look. With everything that's happened we haven't even considered names. I'm still partly in shock I'm now a father.

"That can wait until after the ceremony," my father cuts in before any of us can say a word.

Frowning, I watch him hand my son to my mother. She's cooing over the little ones with the enthusiasm of a doting grandmother.

"What ceremony?" I ask.

Coventina rescues the other twin from Fontus, who's wearing the same confused expression as I am. The next thing I know, there's a flash of light, and we find ourselves standing on a deserted stretch of golden beach. Sapphire waters lap at the sand, and a warm breeze plays with my hair. The evening sky above is painted in reds, pinks, and golds as the sun sets on the horizon. It's not Italy, of that I'm certain. Somewhere in the Caribbean is my guess.

Eva and Fontus are beside me. Behind us, the rest of the family stands gathered in a group. Neptune himself is waiting for us on the beach with an entourage from his ocean court.

"We are gathered here to see the three of you bound in matrimony," Jupiter informs us, his expression daring me to argue. "There have only ever been three triads in existence to my knowledge. Your binding has made you powerful yet vulnerable. There is a balance you must maintain for you and it to survive. Together you will be a valuable asset in our fight against Pluto. An asset we cannot allow to fade. You must therefore complete the links you have already forged. Commit to each other fully and forever as mates."

Taking Eva's hand, I draw her to me and look down into her beautiful face. Her lips are parted, and her brown hair tumbles loosely around her shoulders as her large eyes stare up at me trustingly. Then reaching for Fontus, I tug him in beside her, admiring his bronzed skin and muscled physique. His gaze is just as accepting.

"If Eva's father is anything like my own, we aren't being given a choice here," I inform them gently. "But I won't agree to wed you both unless I know that's what you want, and, Eva, even if you do agree, but you want something more splendid, we can wait."

Eva gently cups my jaw, her fingers caressing my face. "Apollo, we love you. Where you go now, we follow. I know everything has happened too fast, but perhaps, that's how it was meant to be. I want to marry you both. Here. Now. This is perfect for me, and I wouldn't want to change a thing."

Fontus nods in agreement, raising my hand to press a loving kiss to my knuckles. "A god's heart is never fickle. When we find the one or ones we're supposed to be with, there's no stopping us from being together."

Wrapping my arms around them both lovingly, I share a passionate kiss with each. "I love both of you. You've become more than life itself for me. I'd die to protect you. Nothing on Earth will ever change that."

Never once did I think my future would be found in the sea. Yet here they are. Eva and Fontus. Two young hearts willing to beat alongside my own for eternity.

"Let's get on with it," Neptune booms. "I want to meet my grandsons properly and begin the celebrations."

Eva rolls her eyes at her father, but the smile on her lips is filled with happiness.

Standing among family and friends, we speak the vows of love. Our hands are bound to each other's by silken white cord in a traditional hand-fastening ceremony. The sun continues to set, casting us all in its golden glow. Seeing them watching me so lovingly steals my breath. My thoughts turn to tonight … our wedding night. When we're finally alone, I'm going to make love to every inch of both of them. Worship them with everything I am.

As the rite comes to an end, a cheer goes up.

I get lost in kissing Eva and Fontus, and the lust I taste on both their mouths is a promise of the night ahead.

We're quickly ushered back to my father's villa where the servants have set out a feast in our honor. Love, laughter, and merriment follow. The trials of the island are dimmed but not forgotten and nor is Pluto's evil scheme. With other islands and captives to discover, we'll have our work cut out for us.

Toasts are made. Wine is drunk, and food is consumed. At some point Mars and his wife scurry off, no doubt intending to find some privacy to have fun.

Leaving my father's side, I head over to Eva. Fussing over the twins, she has Coventina and my mother aiding her.

"I think we should call it an early night," I inform her, wiggling my eyebrows.

Looping a lock of hair behind her ear, her cheeks heat with a pretty shade of pink.

"The babies…."

"Coventina and I can look after them, tonight," my mother assures her with a gentle touch to her arm. "Go enjoy your husbands. There will be time enough to worry about your boys tomorrow."

I give my mother a wink, thankful she's kind enough to look after them and also aware she's hoping for more grand-children soon. Her life has been empty of little ones to play with since we all grew up. I know she longs for the next generation to watch over.

Lacing my fingers in Eva's, I guide her away from the women and in search of Fontus. The party will continue long into dawn. These things can even run for days in my family. By the time we wake, I'm more than sure we'll be caught up in a second round of celebrations as our guests drink my father's wine cellars dry. Even Neptune looks like he's having a good time and is not about to leave any time soon.

We find Fontus with my sister. Diana looks bored as he chats away beside her. From her expression, I doubt she'll stay at the villa much longer. She's always been a loner, preferring open spaces.

"Fontus, come. It's time for bed," I tell him with a command that makes Eva shiver beside me.

Sliding off his seat, he eagerly hurries to take my offered hand. His grip is warm and sure as it finds mine. With no threats or danger hanging over us, I know tonight will be one we won't forget in a hurry.

My sister raises her glass in a salute. "Congratulations, Brother. Let's hope your offspring aren't as irritating as their father."

A chuckle escapes my lips at her comment. "Wait until it's your turn,"

Diana scrunches up her nose. "Never going to happen."

Leading my husband and wife toward the stairs to the room above, which has been specially prepared for us, I remember Fontus' words on the beach. 'A god's heart is never fickle. When we find the one or ones we're supposed to be with, there's no stopping us from being together.' He's right. This was always meant to be. An island filled with beasts, magic, death, and even the God of the Underworld himself couldn't stop us. The forces that brought us together could not be denied. Our hearts knew even before our heads.

I've been blessed.

My being is full, and I know with Eva and Fontus at my side we're capable of overcoming anything we're faced with in the future.

If you plan to continue with this series, there's an epilogue...but I suggest you stop here if you don't like cliffhangers and don't plan to continue.

Thanks for reading!

RIVER

Epilogue

I allow the massive wings on my back to close, and I swoop down onto the burned ground of the mountain. Having landed on my hind lion feet first, my eagle claws at the front touch down and embed into the still warm earth. The air is thick with the stench of fire. It catches in my throat and brings a squawk of annoyance from it. I only flew over here a few days ago, and it was a green and colorful place, full of fruit and life. I don't understand what's happened. The magic I felt has also gone. It was the most powerful energy to have ever hit me. It was lust filled but sad at the same time. There was a sorrow so great that its heaviness pulled on the island.

Was this the place my pack were disappearing to? If so, all evidence will have been destroyed.

I'm the alpha of a pack of all sorts, as we put it. Mythological creatures from the stories of old hidden away together in the mountains of central Europe where we can't be discovered. We have a variety of different creatures living among us from centaurs to pegasus horses. I'm a griffon. We're not thought of as the pleasantest of beasts, but that's old fashioned myths and legends for you. One of our kind does something wrong, and our reputation is destroyed forever. My front half is the body of an eagle and my back half's that of a lion. Griffons have a feared reputation, but although my rule within my pack is a powerful one, I'm not a coldhearted killer like many people believe my species to be. Well, unless you're a small rabbit, then if you don't outrun me, you'll end up as my dinner. We don't spend all our time in our mythological form. Over the years, we've adapted and have developed a human side. My human state is a brown-haired, brown-eyed man with a thing for tattoos—I can't get enough of them. Thankfully they don't show when I shift.

Jumping down the mountain some distance, I look for anything that could help me discover the truth of what happened here. Sniffing the air, I hope to find clues, but everything here is dead.

"Damn it!" I cry, and the words come out as the screech of an angry eagle.

Taking off again, I allow the winds swirling around the island to carry me higher and farther away from the warmth of the nearby volcano—the source of the eruption that destroyed the island. It seems too convenient for it to erupt when I was getting so close to finding the pack members who've disappeared.

Among those we've lost is a female human—she's the only one in our pack. We grew up together as brother and sister despite our obvious differences. Fern was abandoned as a baby, and my parents took her into their care. One day she went for a walk and never came back. I've been searching for her ever since. I should have flown down and searched when I came here last week, but something about the emotion of the island scared me off. I didn't want to believe she was here, because it felt so beautiful but also so painful. I will find her, and when I do, I'll destroy everyone who's had a hand in taking her.

The path of the jet-black lava flow leads down to the sea where having reached the salt water it stops. It looks almost magical as if the sea has rejected the fiery, molten hell of destruction. A glint from among the lava covered scenery captures my attention, and I dive toward it in an instant. The ground isn't as hot here. When I land, I shift back into my human form. The heat of the sun on my back instantly hits me. It's reflecting off the rocks and is causing the temperature to rise. Nothing will come back to life in this place. It will forever be known as hell. Hell ... that's what it must have felt like last week. The devil possessed this place and burned it alive. People, creatures, they all would have died here. Maybe Fern too. We've had several regular shifters disappear: lions and bears. I don't know why I'm feeling the way I do, because Griffons aren't known for their empathic powers, but I feel agony here. Agony and birth. It's a toxic mix that leaves me breathless. People have died here and in ways I don't want to think about.

I need to discover what was glittering before I'm weighed down by the desolate atmosphere of this island—it weighs too heavy for anyone to survive here for long. Hell. It really is Hell. I look around until I spot the sparkling object once again. Bending down, I reach for it, and pulling hard, I retrieve an arrowhead from the lava. It wasn't fully covered, and having removed it, I realize why. It was buried in a person whose body has been forever preserved by the lava.

What the hell happened in this place?

Holding the arrowhead up, I take a closer look at it. There's an inscription on it, but I can't make out what it says. I grasp it in my hand and search for any other clues. On closer inspection, this entire area appears to have been a battle field and not that long ago.

Who fought here? Was Fern among them? I'd like to think I'd sense the presence of my surrogate sister if she was buried under the wasteland this beach has now become. I can't though. It fills me with hope that maybe she's still alive somewhere.

Transforming back into a griffon, I clasp the arrowhead tightly between my talons and fly around the island one more time. There's nothing else here. The place is barren now. I have the only clue I'm going to get—the arrowhead. I just need to find out who it belongs to and discover what they know about this place that feels like Hell on Earth.

The End

* * *

The Gods Reborn series will continue with Diana's Pride - Out January 2020.

AFTERWORD

Apollo's Protection will be exclusively available in Prophecy of Magic until November 2019

Dangerous fates, mysterious curses, twisted fairy tales, and doomed prophecies...
Explore new worlds in Prophecy of Magic: a collection of over twenty urban fantasy and paranormal romance novels curated especially for the genre's biggest fans!
Don't miss the chance to hold magic in your hand. One-click your copy today!

https://www.prophecyofmagic.com/

Beauty's War by Anna Edwards & Claire Marta. Gods Reborn, Book One.

Vicky thought she knew who she was — a young woman from Devon, England with a love of drawing. However, a trip to Rome reveals there are ancient forces at work, which she never knew existed. Beauty in her world is dying. Can a handsome stranger save her from the encroaching darkness and allow her to find her true self before it is too late?

Mars is the God of War and Masculinity. If he wants something, he takes it, that is the force he wields in a world blinded to his existence. The enemy has arrived, and a war is coming. Can he find the control he needs to overcome evil or will his feelings toward a human woman bring him to his knees?

The power of the gods and their eternal battle of good vs. evil is about to be unleashed on an unsuspecting world. Is it possible for

Mars to reawaken Venus before the God of the Underworld captures them in his deadly trap?

Beauty's War is a dark modern day, fantasy, paranormal romance based upon Roman mythology.

You shouldn't always believe the history you were taught, because the reality may be something completely unexpected.

CLAIRE

A native Brit, I live in Italy with my husband and daughter. When I am not writing and drinking copious amounts of tea, I enjoy taking photos of my adoptive country, trying to stay fit with running, reading amazing books and being a stay at home mother.

CONNECT WITH CLAIRE MARTA
https://clairemartawritesbooks.wordpress.com
Newsletter: https://clairemartawritesbooks.
wordpress.com/contact/
Email: clare.marta@aol.com

Paranormal Romance - The Hunter Chronicles Series

- Frostbite
- Dark Desires
- Claimed by Magic
- The Serpent's Kiss
- Twitch
- Blood Moon Rising

Dark Paranormal Romance - Ceasefire Series

- The Devil You Know
- The Devil's Plaything
- From Ashes and Embers

Standalone

- His Salvation – Cavalieri Della Morte, Standalone

ANNA

I am a British author, from the depths of the rural country-side near London. When I have some spare time, I can also be found writing poetry, baking cakes (and eating them), or behind a camera snapping like a mad paparazzi. I'm an avid reader who turned to writing to combat my depression and anxiety. I have a love of travelling and like to bring this to my stories to give them the air of reality. I like my heroes hot and hunky with a dirty mouth, my heroines demure but with spunk, and my books full of dramatic suspense.

CONNECT WITH ANNA EDWARDS
www.AuthorAnnaEdwards.com
Newsletter: http://eepurl.com/cwxJ6v
Email: anna1000edwards@gmail.com

Paranormal Romance - The Glacial Blood Series

- The Touch of Snow
- Fighting the Lies
- Fallen for Shame
- Shattered Fears
- Hidden Pain

Romantic Suspense - The Control Series

- Surrendered Control
- Divided Control
- Misguided Control
- Controlling Darkness
- Controlling Heritage
- Controlling Disgrace
- Controlling Expectations
- Controlling the Past
- The Control Series Boxset

Dark Romance - Dark Sovereignty

- Legacy of Succession
- Tainted Reasoning
- A Father's Insistence

Standalones

- Oliver - Part of Blaire's World
- Redemption - Book Ten of the Cavalieri Della Torte
- Overexposed - A Skeleton Kings Prequel

Printed in Poland
by Amazon Fulfillment
Poland Sp. z o.o., Wrocław